Titles By Laurel Osterkamp

Following My Toes
Starring in the Movie of My Life
The Holdout
The Next Breath
The Standout
Just Like the Bronte Sisters
Favorite Daughters
Beautiful Little Furies
Murder at Styles Resort

MURDER At Styles Resort

Adapted from
The Mysterious Event at Styles
by Agatha Christie

LAUREL OSTERKAMP

ISBN: 978-1-933826-74-5

PUBLISHED BY DRAMA, DRAMA, and imprint of PMI BOOKS. Boulder, CO.

Contents

ONE

I GO TO STYLES

Of course, social media went crazy over the murder of Emily Styles-Cavendish. When a rich, older woman gets poisoned by a family member, every true crime fan has a theory. I know beyond the shadow of a doubt, that they arrested the guilty person. Yet, murder has a stench, and those of us who witnessed Emily die carried that stench, even though we were all innocent. That's why both Perle and Emily's family asked me to write what actually went down. Maybe then the world could move on and talk about something else.

Thus, I will share with you all the sordid details, and I'll try to stay on-topic. But I'm only human, and I might occasionally give you some personal context as well. It's the only way the story will make sense.

First, if there hadn't been a riot at the state capitol, I wouldn't have been involved in the whole mess. But people were angry, angrier than normal, and some of the extremely disgruntled ones felt compelled to express their ire by yelling and breaking things and threatening members of the Minnesota State Legislature. It was my job, as a security officer, to keep the peace. But as a *female* security officer, I was an easy target, and one rioter caused me to fall down the marble staircase and hit my head. I suffered a concussion. They put me on a mandatory medical leave for six weeks, even though I insisted I was fine.

The timing was good, though. The legislature was about to go into recess. That's when state Senator John Cavendish called me. He was one of my very favorite senators, and boy, could he make a compelling floor speech. "Helen," he said, "I hope you don't mind me calling you on your cell."

"How'd you get my number?"

He laughed. "I pulled a few strings."

It made sense. John Cavendish never met a stranger. He was friends with everyone at work, including the near-humans in HR. If anyone could pull strings, it was John Cavendish.

"What can I do for you, John?" I asked him.

"No, no. The question, Helen, is what can I do for you? You saved my life, you know."

"You're exaggerating."

After all, the rioters hadn't been set on killing anyone. But John, a Democrat, had recently voted to uphold Covid restrictions. He also supported the protesters of racial inequities and he championed social justice. John was a target that day, and some of the truly scary rioters called him out by name. When I stepped between him and a dude sporting a red bandana and a denim vest, he waved an aluminum baseball bat meant to collide with John's head, but it hit me instead. That caused my fall.

"I'm not exaggerating," John now answered, "and I want to repay you somehow." He cleared his throat, sounding uneasy. "Look, Helen, I don't mean to pry. But I heard your concussion wasn't the main reason for your leave."

My defenses went up. "What do you mean? Who told you that?"

Like a true politician, he evaded the question. "We're all on your side. After what you've been through, anyone would need time to heal, both physically and emotionally. Do you have someone looking after you?"

John knew the answer to that. Two years ago, when I started work at the state capitol, I was a newlywed. Once, on a coffee break, I showed John my wedding photos. Me in my white dress, beaming and in love, my husband Paul looking at me with adoration. "You make a beautiful couple," John had said.

Perhaps he was just being nice, but Paul and I looked good together—sort of. We both had athletic builds, with skin that tanned easily and shiny brown hair. Luckily, Paul's bright blue eyes and tall stature saved us from looking like siblings, since I was merely five-four, and my eyes were an everyday brown. I always thought Paul was a bit too handsome for me, that people would glance at us and deem him out of my league.

Eventually, I came to realize that anyone who thought that was right.

It didn't happen right away. First, I became pregnant, and John was the person at work who I told. "I am so excited," I'd said, "but I hope they don't hold it against me. A pregnant security guard could be a liability."

"That would be illegal, to hold it against you," John said. He sat at his desk, wearing a V-neck cashmere sweater with a shirt and tie underneath. His brown hair, graying at the temples, swept over his forehead in the perfect arc. "If they give you any trouble, come to me."

I thanked him and promised that I would. But several weeks later, I miscarried. I was out for three days, and when I returned, I knocked on his office door and, holding back tears, said, "So, I'm no longer pregnant. Please don't mention it to anyone, okay?"

John's eyes pooled with sympathy. He said simply, "Of course. Are you alright?"

"Yes," I stated. I had to be okay. It was my job to make his workplace secure.

Six months later, the other shoe dropped. Paul left me for someone else. That time, I didn't tell John anything, but he must have heard through the grapevine. Suddenly and for no reason, he would bring me my favorite coffee—Americana with a shot of hazelnut syrup—from the cafe downstairs, and when there were fresh-baked cookies, he'd bring me those as well.

Now, on the phone, I responded. "I'm on my own. But I'm fine."

"I have a proposition for you. My stepmother owns that resort up in Lutsen. It's the off-season. You should come stay."

Lutsen, Minnesota is a resort town along the north shore of Lake Superior. There's a rash of state parks up that way, with waterfalls and picturesque hiking trails. Summer and fall were their busiest seasons, though winter brought skiers and snow-shoers brave enough to face the cold. But early spring, when the ground was soggy, and the trees were still bare, was their slow time.

Yet, nothing could take away from the beauty of Lake Superior, and I'd heard about how fancy the Styles Resort was. In fact, when Paul and I got married, we'd thought about honeymooning there, but we didn't have the funds. We went cabin camping instead.

"Don't tell me you have no guests," I stated. "There are always people who want to stay at Styles."

"Honestly, we're going through a phase right now."

"A phase?"

John's sigh communicated his unease, even over the phone. "My stepmother recently remarried a guy who is much younger than she is. He's actually closer in age to me and my brother Lawrence. There's been tension about how we should run things. So, Lawrence, my wife Mary, and I are all going to stay over the next few weeks to try and figure it out. Styles will be closed to guests. You'd be doing me a favor, Helen, if you came to stay too. Your presence could help lighten the mood."

I did not ask how I, who was still recovering from both a head trauma and the emotional rollercoaster of the last sixteen months, would lighten the mood. John only said that because that's what socially generous people did; they convinced you that you were doing them a favor, when really, the reverse was true.

Aside from that, I'd seen photos of the Styles Resort in Lutsen. There was a pool house, a glorious dining room with a golden wood interior, and cozy bedrooms, each with a lake view and its own fireplace. That beat the prospect of me sitting alone in my one-bedroom apartment, a flood of regret as my only companion.

"If you're sure I wouldn't be imposing ..." I said.

"Not at all. Emily, my stepmother, will love you."

"What's she like?"

John explained how Emily had married John's father when he was a widower with two sons, and she'd always been warm, vibrant, and generous, and all his friends remarked how she was younger and more beautiful than their moms were. "She's now in her mid-sixties, but she looks and acts a lot younger, so I guess it's not a surprise that she'd marry someone who only just turned fifty."

John told me that his father and Emily had purchased the Styles Resort early in their married life, and they gave it Emily's maiden name, since a lot of the money came from Emily's rather large trust. Before John's father died, he willed his share of the place to her for her lifetime, as well as the larger part of his income; an arrangement that was sort of unfair to his two sons. Not that John complained. "Emily has always been so generous to Lawrence and me. In fact, we were so young when she married Dad that we always thought of her as our own mother."

He told me about how she put Lawrence through medical school. And that she never said a word when he decided that rather than being a doctor, he'd live at the resort and try to find success as a novelist.

"She put me through law school too," said John. "So, I don't begrudge her any of the inheritance from my dad. But we're all financially and emotionally invested in the Styles Resort, so I'll admit it: I'm not crazy about this new husband of hers. He has a lot of opinions."

"How did they meet?"

"He's Evie's cousin."

John said this like I should know who Evie was. But then, as if he could sense my confusion, he went on. "Evie is the property manager. She's great. Super energetic and capable, and she and Emily have become best friends. But one day, her cousin Alfred showed up from nowhere. Evie didn't seem happy to see him."

I thought of my family, which was incredibly small. I had no experience with estranged relatives because my relatives are few. "She didn't want to see her own cousin?" I asked.

"He's, well …" John sighed. "I hate to say it, but the guy is strange. He's got this long, thick blond beard, and he looks like he inherited only recessive genes."

I laughed despite myself. "Okay, but that's not his fault."

"No, but we all have a choice in how we present ourselves. There's the beard, and his John Lennon glasses, and he wears patent leather boots, even in the snow! But he and Emily instantly hit it off, and she offered him a job doing odd jobs and bookkeeping. Then, three months ago, she suddenly announced that she and Alfred had eloped! 'It was a spontaneous decision, but I've never been happier,' she told us. Lawrence and I think he's after her money, but we can't tell her that. She's way too strong-willed to hear it."

"It must be a difficult situation for you."

"Difficult! It's awful!" He took a deep breath and cleared his throat. "Sorry. If I don't watch myself, I'll scare you away from coming."

The opposite was true. I've always felt more comfortable helping others than with letting them help me. Besides, I'd learned some investigative skills while taking my criminology coursework, and now I was itching to use them. Perhaps I could dig up some dirt on this Alfred and help John out.

Three days later, I drove my beat-up little Volvo from St. Paul to Lutsen. John was concerned that I wasn't well enough to drive myself, but I assured him I'd be fine. When I pulled up to the beautiful red multiplex set against the rich evergreens, John came out to meet me.

"Welcome, Helen!" John, handsome and outdoorsy in his LL Bean gear, fit perfectly into the surroundings. "How was the drive?"

I looked out at the landscape, with the rocky shore of Lake Superior, the sky like a shiny sapphire and blending with the navy depths of the water, and the evergreens so tall and peaceful under the afternoon sun. It seemed almost impossible to believe that, not so very far away, turmoil and partisanship raged, both in the Twin Cities and throughout our nation. It was like I'd been transported into another world.

"My drive was good." I gave him my most enthusiastic smile and then turned to lug my bag out of the trunk of my car.

"Here, let me get that for you." He took my bag and gestured that I should follow him. It felt unnatural, letting him be chivalrous, when normally my job was to protect him. But perhaps I could get used to accepting a bit of help. As we approached the lodge, John said, "I'm afraid it is very quiet up here, Helen."

"That sounds perfect," I responded. "This seems like paradise."

"I'd say that it was paradise, if it weren't for Alfred Inglethorp!" He paused in the doorway and glanced at his watch.

"Is something wrong?"

"Not at all. I'm just not sure if I'm supposed to pick up Cynthia."

"Cynthia? I thought your wife is named Mary."

"No, no. Cynthia is the daughter of one of Emily's old high school friends."

"Does she live with you?" I didn't keep the confusion out of my voice.

"Yeah. Cynthia was an only child, and her parents had her later in life. Sadly, both of Cynthia's parents died in a car accident, and Cynthia was alone. Then she discovered her parents were deeply in debt. Emily came to the rescue, and Cynthia has been with us for nearly two years now. She works in the Grand Marais Medical Center, a few miles away." He swiped on his phone, apparently texting her. A moment later, there was the ding of a response. John smiled. "She doesn't need a ride."

He picked up my bag, and we walked inside. A woman with prematurely silver hair, wearing bohemian-looking overalls, polished the golden wood in the lobby. She straightened herself when we came in.

"Hi Evie, here's the heroic Helen I was telling you about. Helen, this is Evie."

Evie shook hands with a hearty, almost painful, grip. Her blue eyes and her friendly, sunburnt face struck me. She was fit, and I guessed she was about forty, with a deep, almost masculine voice. Plus, she was tall. Her feet seemed to match her height, and they were encased in men's work boots. When she spoke, her gruff tone matched her appearance.

"Shore is still icy. Don't want to slip on the rocks. Better be careful."

"Of course," I responded. "And please let me know how I can help while I'm here. I like to make myself useful."

She chuckled. "You'll regret saying that."

"You're a cynic, Evie." John said, laughing. "Come on then, you deserve a break. Let's eat lunch."

"Well." Evie wiped her hands against her overalls. "I am hungry."

She led the way round to the dining room, where deli platters sat upon tables by a wall covered with a wine rack.

A figure rose from one of the chairs and came a few steps to meet us.

"Helen, this is my wife, Mary."

Mary Cavendish had a tall, slender form and wonderful tawny eyes; she reminded me of a leopard trapped in a house cat's body.

"Helen." She took me in her arms and hugged me tight, which definitely took me by surprise. "Thank you for saving John's life."

"I, umm …" I waited until it wouldn't seem rude to pull away, and then I met her gaze. "I don't know what John told you, but—"

"He described your heroism."

"He was being hyperbolic."

"I doubt that. John isn't creative enough for extreme exaggeration."

My mouth dropped open. How could she insult him like that when he stood right there? I glanced at John, but he seemed unfazed.

"Anyway," Mary continued, "I'm so glad you're here, and I hope there is some way we can repay you."

"I'm happy to be here, too. Thank you for your hospitality."

"Would you like something to drink? Tea? Soda? Wine?"

"Just water. Thank you."

At that moment, a voice floated from down the hall.

"Then you'll contact the art colony about the silent auction? I think we should offer a luxury package."

A male voice murmured softly, and then Emily's voice rose in reply:

"Yes, certainly. Call them after lunch. You are so sweet, Alfred."

There was the sound of footsteps approaching, and then an ageless beauty, with white hair styled into a bob with heavy bangs emphasizing still-bright eyes and a gamine chin, stepped into the dining room. A man followed her, his manner deferential.

Emily greeted me like we were old friends. "Why, Helen! It is delightful to meet the woman who keeps John safe. We can never thank you enough for your service." She took both my hands in hers and squeezed. "You will let me know if there's anything we can do to make your stay more comfortable, yes?"

"Yes, thank you. It is nice to meet you, Mrs. Styles."

"Call me Emily." She looked over her shoulder. "And this is my husband, Alfred. Alfred, darling …" she gestured for him to come forward. "… this is Helen, who you've heard so much about."

I subtly checked out "Alfred darling." No wonder John hated Alfred's facial hair; the beard was long and scraggly, topped by a mustache that made him look like he was in a barbershop quartet. Alfred wore thin-framed John Lennon glasses, and a detached expression. He looked like a sidekick character in a sitcom but seemed out of place in real life. His voice was rather deep and unctuous. He placed a wooden hand in mine and said, "This is a pleasure, Helen." Then, turning to his wife: "Emily dearest, I think it's a bit drafty." He placed over her shoulders a shawl that had been left on a nearby chair.

She gave Alfred a warm, grateful smile, as if he'd just rescued her from peril. What did such a warm, beautiful woman see in him?

With Alfred's mere presence, a cloud of veiled hostility seemed to descend over everyone in the room but Emily. Evie took no pains to conceal her feelings. She kicked at a chair and mumbled something angry and unintelligible.

If Alfred noticed, he didn't let on, and neither did Emily. She invited us all to serve ourselves lunch, and she poured out a steady flood of conversation, mainly about the Grand Marais Art Colony's silent auction. Occasionally, she'd look at Alfred. He gazed at her with an attentive eye that bordered on creepy. Perhaps John had biased me against Alfred, but every time I looked at him, I cringed.

Eventually, Emily gave Evie a list of tasks that needed completing, and they both got up to resume working. Alfred spoke to me.

"After your recovery, will you go back to being a security guard, Helen?"

I tried to hide my visceral reaction toward him and kept my voice light. "Maybe. Or I might make a fresh start."

Mary Cavendish leant forward. "What sort of job would you really choose if you could do anything you wanted?"

I shrugged. The lie slipped out easily. "I don't know."

"Oh, come on. You don't have a fantasy job? Everyone does."

"I suppose I do, but it's silly."

She smiled. "But that's the whole point. Besides, who am I to judge?"

I took a deep breath. "Well, I've always thought it would be fun to be a private investigator."

"The real thing?" She tucked a stray lock of shiny blond hair behind her ear. "Aren't you worried that all your clients would be jealous husbands trying to catch their cheating wives?"

I shrugged. "Possibly. But I took a seminar in private investigating once, when I got my bachelor's degree in criminology. The instructor was this French woman who came to the U.S. for an Ivy League education, and the rumor was that she'd once worked as a spy for the CIA. We became friends, and she told me how she gave up her career to get married and have kids. Well, every semester she teaches one seminar in private investigations at the University of Minnesota, and it is the most competitive class to get into. Anyway, she is one of the smartest people I have ever met. She used to say that all good detective work was a mere matter of method."

"That's fascinating," said Mary. "Would I have heard of her? She sounds like she could be a local celebrity."

"Probably not. But she started a successful lifestyle blog besides being a stay-at-home mom/adjunct professor. She's funny, a tiny woman with this elegance about her, and more energetic than most people half her age. I think she could have been a brilliant detective, had her life gone in a different direction."

"Most people who read detective stories think they have what it takes to be one," said Alfred. Had he heard a word I said?

"I suppose," I answered.

"I like detective stories," continued Alfred stroking his mustache. "But most of the novels written today are trash. The criminal is discovered in the last chapter, and everyone is dumbfounded. With an actual crime, you'd know at once."

"Yeah, but most crimes go unpunished," I argued.

"I'm not talking about the police, but the people who are indirectly involved. The family. You couldn't really fool them. They'd know."

"Then," I said, skeptical, "you think that if you were mixed up in a crime, say a murder, you could spot the murderer right away?"

"I believe I would. Perhaps I couldn't prove it to the authorities. But I'm certain I'd know. I'd feel it in my fingertips if he came near."

"It might be a 'she,'" I suggested.

"True. But murder's a violent crime. We associate it more with a man."

"Poisoning isn't violent." Mary's clear voice startled me. "And Dr. Blake was saying yesterday that, because many medical professionals are ignorant of the effects of many poisons, a lot of cases aren't ever detected."

At that moment, Emily walked back into the room, clearly having heard us. "Jeez, Mary, that's dark!" she cried. "I feel like someone is dancing on my grave. Oh, there's Cynthia!"

A young woman in scrubs walked lightly into the room. "Hello, everyone." Her voice was as light and airy as her appearance, with her rosy complexion and easygoing smile.

For a reason I didn't understand, Emily frowned and used an annoyed tone. "Cynthia, you are late today."

"I had to stay to fill some extra prescriptions."

"Hmph," Emily responded. Then she gestured toward me. "Well, this is Helen. Helen, this is Cynthia."

Cynthia nearly bounced on the soles of her shoes as she untied her hair from its scrunchie. I envied the great loose waves of her auburn hair, and the smallness and whiteness of the hand she held out to greet me. If her eyes and eyelashes were darker, she could have been a model.

"Nice to meet you," she said, her handshake firm.

"Likewise," I said.

She helped herself to a sandwich and sat down next to John.

"I hear you work in the clinic?" I asked.

She nodded. "Actually, I work in the pharmacy."

"How many people do you poison?" I asked, smiling.

Cynthia smiled too. "Oh, hundreds!" she said.

"Cynthia," called Emily, "do you think you could write a few emails for me?"

"Of course, Aunt Emily."

Cynthia jumped up, discarding her uneaten sandwich onto the plate she'd grabbed. It seemed like Cynthia, who'd just finished working at one job, was now beginning her shift at another. Perhaps Emily's generosity came with strings attached.

Emily turned to me.

"John will show you your room. Dinner is at seven. Again, let me know anything you need at all."

"Thank you," I said to her back, as she was already walking away.

"Come with me, Helen," John said. He took me through the lodge and up the broad staircase, which forked right and left half-way to different wings of the building. My room was in the left wing and looked out over the lake.

John left me, and a few minutes later, I saw him from my window, strolling across the beach, arm in arm with Cynthia. I heard Emily call for her impatiently, and then Cynthia quickly ran back to the house. At the same moment, a man stepped out from the shadow of a tree and trudged in the same direction. He looked about forty, very dark and intense, with a clean-shaven face. Some violent emotion seemed to own him. He looked up at my window as he passed, and I guessed it was John's younger brother, Lawrence Cavendish.

What was his deal?

Then I shook off my concern and decided I could use a nap. The bed was soft, with a down comforter and many pillows, and I let the sound of the wind rattling at the windows lull me into the best sleep I'd had in ages.

The next day, the morning dawned bright and sunny. Mary suggested we go for a hike, and we chose a trail that led to a waterfall. When we returned to the lodge at around noon, John beckoned us both into the lounge. His face was obviously full of bad news. We followed him in, and he shut the door after us.

"You missed all the drama, Mary. Evie and Alfred got into an argument, and Evie quit."

Mary's mouth dropped open. "Evie quit?"

John nodded gloomily.

"Yes; she went to tell Emily, and—oh, here's Evie herself."

Evie entered the lounge. She pressed her lips together in a grim expression, and she carried a small suitcase. She looked excited and ready to defend herself.

"I had to say it!" she burst out, "And I told her the truth!"

"Evie, you're leaving?" Mary asked, seemingly in shock.

Evie crossed her arms over her chest. "It's time. I said some things to Emily that she won't forgive or forget in a hurry. I told her, 'You're no spring chicken, Emily, and there's no fool like an old fool. The man's nearly twenty years younger than you, and you shouldn't kid yourself. He married you for money! I hate to say it, but Alfred would murder you in your bed if he thought he'd benefit from it. He's sketchy. You can say what you like to me, but remember what I've told you. He's sketchy.'"

Mary gasped. "What did Emily say?"

Evie's face fell into a grim scowl. "She called me a liar. She said I was jealous because I don't have a husband, and she's had two. And that I had some family grudge against Alfred that she would not try to understand. Then she told me to pack my things and go."

"Can't you wait a few hours so you can both cool off?" John asked.

"No. It must be this minute!"

For a moment, we sat and stared at her. Finally, John stood. "I'm going to talk to Emily."

"I'll join you," Mary said.

As they left the room, Evie's face changed. She leant toward me eagerly.

"Helen, you seem honest. I can trust you?"

I had the urge to run and hide when she laid her hand on my arm. Her voice sank to a whisper.

"Look after her, Helen. My poor Emily. They're a lot of sharks—all of them. I know what I'm talking about. Each person at Styles wants her money. I've protected her as much as I could. Now that I'm out of the way, she's in real danger."

"Of course, Evie," I said. "I'll do everything I can, but I'm sure you're just upset. After all, Alfred is your family. And I can't imagine that John and Mary–"

She interrupted me by slowly shaking her forefinger.

"Please, Helen. Believe me. Trust me. I've lived longer than you. Please, keep your eyes open. You'll see what I mean."

Evie rose and moved to the door. Grasping the handle, she turned her head over her shoulder and called to me.

"Above all, Helen, watch that devil—her husband!"

By the time John had returned from talking with Emily, Evie was gone. "She left without saying goodbye?" he asked.

"She was determined to get out of here," I answered.

He sighed. "I could use some air. Do you want to go for a walk?"

I'd only just returned from a walk, but since John clearly wanted company, I agreed. We went outside and strolled around the grounds. "Hey guys," Cynthia called. She ran to join us. "What happened with Evie?"

As we walked, John filled her in. I spotted a man in the distance. He walked with his head bowed and his shoulders hunched. "Who's that?" I asked. "I thought you didn't have any guests."

"That's Dr. Blake," said John shortly.

"And who is Dr. Blake?"

"He's staying in one of our condos, rebounding after a nasty divorce where his wife got everything. Apparently, he's a Minneapolis specialist, a very bright man—one of the greatest living experts on poisons, I believe."

"And he and Mary are close," said Cynthia.

John frowned and changed the subject. "I can't believe Evie left on such bad terms. She can be blunt, for sure, but she and Emily have been such good friends."

He took the path over a red-roofed bridge which is often showcased in Style's publicity photos, and from there, we walked into Lutsen's town center, which had a main street lined with coffee shops, a drugstore, a few restaurants, and an antique market.

As we ambled down the sidewalk, a striking woman with a wide smile met John's eyes and gave him a brief nod.

"She seems friendly," I remarked.

John's face hardened. "That is Janet Raikes."

"Her husband died recently," said Cynthia. "It was very unexpected and tragic."

"How awful for her," I replied. For a recent widow, she seemed to be in a great mood, but I kept that thought to myself.

"She's suffered," said John, as if he could read my mind, and with rather unnecessary abruptness.

Suddenly, a vague chill of foreboding crept over me. I brushed it aside.

"Styles Resort is really beautiful," I said to John. "Thanks again for inviting me."

He nodded rather gloomily. "Yes, we're very proud of Styles Resort. But for the last few years, it's been losing money. I've been sinking my inheritance into it, even though I don't officially own any part of the property. Mary says I'm stupid to do so, that it's why I'm so cash poor as I am now."

"Do you mean you're in debt?"

"Oh Helen, you don't even want to know."

"Couldn't your brother help you?"

"Lawrence? He's made no money. Being a self-published author with a medical degree doesn't pay much, not if you don't use that degree. It would be fine, him living off Emily, except now Alfred is doing the same thing. Where does that leave me?"

Cynthia squeezed his arm as they continued to walk. "Come on," she said. "Let's get a cappuccino." She pointed to one of the coffee shops, and they headed over, with me following.

I thought about Evie. It seemed her presence at Style Resort had given the place a sense of security. With her gone, that security was removed—and the air seemed rife with suspicion. Now this Dr. Blake guy added to that feeling. My mind felt invaded by shadows, and for just for a moment, I had a premonition of approaching evil.

TWO

POISON, ARGUMENTS, AND DR. DOOM

I settled into Styles Resort and relaxed. I spent most of my time staring out at Lake Superior. It soothed my soul while reminding me of my personal insignificance, but comfortingly. I also read trashy novels and went on daily hikes. John and Cynthia were especially nice, and I soon grew to think of them as friends. I didn't see too much of Alfred, which was a relief. Mary was around, but Dr. Blake monopolized a lot of her time. I'd given him my private nickname of "Dr. Doom," as he had huge, dark circles underneath his eyes, and a sagging, white face. He seemed to walk with a constant rain cloud hovering over his head. I'd often catch him lurking in a doorway or staring out a window, waiting for Mary so they could go for a walk or sit in the lounge and talk for hours about who knows what. Just the thought of him sent a shiver down my spine.

Conversely, once I got to know John's brother Lawrence, he didn't seem menacing at all, not like he had at first. One afternoon, we went into Grand Marais for lunch and to stroll around the various art galleries that the small town housed. "We should stop at the clinic and see if Cynthia can take a break," Lawrence suggested. "She's working in the pharmacy today."

"Sounds good," I replied.

Cynthia wore a white jacket over her scrubs, and she greeted us with enthusiasm. "Hi! Let me show you around." She took us to where they filled the prescriptions.

"Look at all these drugs!" I exclaimed, as my eye traveled around the small room. "Have you ever thought about pushing them on the street?"

"Say something original," groaned Cynthia. "Everyone says that, or they joke about how many people I poison. But if people only knew how easy it is to poison someone by mistake, they wouldn't joke about it."

Had she forgotten that I'd joked about her poisoning people when we first met? My cheeks burned at the thought, and all I could think to say was, "That's awful."

She sighed. Then, as if by magic, a smile spread across her face. "I'm starving. Come on, let's go eat."

Lawrence walked toward a big locked cabinet. "Is this where you keep the good stuff?"

"No, Lawrence—that's the cabinet with the potentially lethal drugs. The big cabinet is where we store the narcotics. Not that I'll unlock either for you."

"Damn you, Cynthia." He scowled at her and raised an eyebrow, clearly joking.

I rarely saw this side of Lawrence. Compared to John, Lawrence was difficult to get to know. He was the opposite of his brother in almost every way, being unusually shy and reserved. Yet he was charming in his own way, with a sly smile and large, dark eyes that weren't afraid to gaze into your own. I noticed that Lawrence and

Cynthia could be shy around each other, but when they relaxed into each other's company, they were like two goofy kids.

When we'd paid for lunch and were lingering over the last of our freshly squeezed lemonade, I decided to give Lawrence and Cynthia a bit of alone time. "I think I'll check out the gift shop next door," I told them. "Come find me when you're ready."

They were in the middle of laughing over some inside joke and barely noticed my departure. No matter. I wanted to see the sundries next door; the shop promised organic soap and candles, and hand-knit scarves. As I swung the door open, I nearly ran into a petite woman on her way out. I drew aside and apologized, when suddenly, with a loud exclamation, she clasped me in her arms and kissed me on the cheek.

"*Mon ami* Helen!" she cried. "It is you!"

"Perle!" I exclaimed.

It was my old college instructor/friend, Perle. She had an Ivy League education in—well, I'm not sure what her degree was in—but since graduate school, she became a hyper-organized housewife who ran her own blog, *Ivy League Organizer,* where she shared her lifestyle and parenting tips. She taught one course a semester at the U of M, and in addition, she completed her private investigating (PI) license. There were whispers she used to be a spy, and that made her PI course at the U of M overwhelmingly popular.

On the first day, she told the class, "To understand crime, you must understand yourself. We all might commit foul play in an extreme situation. Realize the predisposition in yourself, and you'll be able to see it in others."

It was a rather dark sentiment, especially in contrast to the source. Perle was hardly over five feet, but she carried herself with impeccable posture, like a former ballerina. (She admitted to once briefly studying at the Paris Opera Ballet.) Her head was perfectly shaped with a bun atop her head, and it sat upon a long, swan-like neck, always perched a little on one side. Her hair appeared lush and dark, but had one silver streak.

"What are you doing in Grand Marais?" I asked.

"Research for my blog," Perle answered.

At that moment, Lawrence and Cynthia arrived. "Perle," said Cynthia. "I didn't realize you'd arrived."

Perle took both of Cynthia's hands into hers. "Yes, yes. I got in this morning. After a lovely little lunch, I drove into town and had a look."

"You two know each other?" I asked.

"Only a little," said Cynthia. "I'm a big fan of Perle's blog, and I convinced Emily that we should have her stay for free, in exchange for publicity on *Ivy League Organizer.*"

Perle beamed at Cynthia. "My kids are both in college, and I figured, why not?" She turned toward me. "*Mon ami* Helen. It has been too long. You are well?"

Perle and I stayed in touch mostly through social media and via email. She knew what I'd been through recently, but we hadn't talked face to face for some time. I shrugged. "More or less. I am staying at Styles as well. I know John Cavendish from the state capital."

"But that is wonderful. I will catch up with my prized student!"

I basked in her praise. We promised to find each other back at Styles later, and Cynthia, Lawrence, and I headed back.

On the ride home, I told them everything I could about Perle. "She really is extraordinary. But she's the ultimate neat freak. Like, a speck of dust would cause her more pain than a bullet wound, so don't be surprised if she educates the staff about their housekeeping methods. And her mind is as sharp as a tack. I doubt there is any puzzle she couldn't figure out."

We arrived back in a very cheerful mood. As we entered the hall, Emily came out, looking flushed and upset.

"Oh, it's you," she said.

"Is there anything the matter, Aunt Emily?" asked Cynthia.

"Certainly not," Emily replied sharply. "Why should there be?" Then, catching sight of Dorcas, the maid, going into the dining room, she called to her to bring some tea into her office.

"Yes, of course." Dorcas hesitated, then added diffidently: "You're looking exhausted. Perhaps you'd like the tea in your bedroom instead?"

"Perhaps you're right, Dorcas—yes—no, not now. There are some emails I must finish today. Have you lit the fire in my room as I told you?"

"Yes."

"Then I'll go to bed directly after supper."

She went into the office again, and Cynthia stared after her.

"Good God! I wonder what's up?" she said to Lawrence.

He did not seem to have heard her, for without a word he turned on his heel and went out of the house.

I suggested a quick swim in the lodge's pool and, Cynthia agreeing, I ran upstairs to change.

Mary was coming down the stairs, wearing her heavy green work shirt over a neat black blouse and skinny jeans. It may have been my imagination, but she, too, was looking odd and disturbed.

"Did you have a good walk with Dr. Blake?" I asked, trying not to let my feelings about him show.

"I didn't go," she replied abruptly. "Where is Emily?"

"In the office."

Her hand clenched itself on the banisters. Then she seemed to steel herself for some encounter, and shot past me down the stairs across the hall to the office, the door of which she shut behind her.

As I ran out to the swimming pool a few moments later, I had to pass the open office window, and could not help overhearing a heated conversation between Mary and Emily.

Emily sounded like she could barely hold in her rage when she said, "Then you won't show it to me?"

"Mary, the two things are unrelated."

"Then show it to me."

Emily sighed. "But it's not what you think, and it has nothing to do with you."

With rising bitterness, Mary replied, "Right. I should have known you'd try to protect him."

Self-conscious to be standing underneath an open window in nothing but my bathing suit, I scurried off to the pool hall. A blast of humid air greeted me. Cynthia was already in the pool, treading water. She greeted me eagerly and said, "Helen, you won't believe it. There's been a terrible argument! Dorcas told me."

"What kind of argument?"

"Between Emily and Alfred. I hope she kicks him out!"

"Was Dorcas there, then?"

Cynthia laughed. "No. She 'happened to be near the door.' She only heard bits and pieces. I wish I knew everything that went down."

I stayed silent and swam and in lazy circles while Cynthia exhausted every plausible hypothesis, and cheerfully hoped, "Emily will send him away, and she will never speak to him again."

Later, after my swim and I'd changed back into jeans and a sweatshirt, I was anxious to find John, but he was nowhere to be seen. Something big had obviously happened that afternoon, and I felt I should warn him. I did not know about the true nature of Emily's arguments with either Mary or Alfred, but John deserved to know whatever I could tell him.

It wasn't John, but Alfred, who I saw when I came down to supper. His face was impassive as ever, and his unreal nature made my skin crawl.

"Is Perle joining us?" I asked no one in particular.

"She is staying in one of our condos with its own kitchen," said

Cynthia. "I believe she wants to cook for herself."

Emily came down last. She still looked flushed, and her eyes never focused on one person or thing for very long. During the meal, there was an awkward silence. Alfred was unusually quiet. He was attentive to Emily, placing a cushion at her back, and altogether playing the part of the devoted husband. Immediately after supper, Emily went to her office again.

"Send my tea in here, Mary," she called. "I'm going to print a few documents."

The Cavendish/Styles/Inglethorp family strongly believed in a cup of green tea after dinner. Emily ordered a specific type from India, and she swore by stirring in a bit of sugar. She said that sugar helped your body absorb the catechins that were in the tea, and that helped your body fight heart disease, stroke, cancer, diabetes, or just about any health condition. I tried the tea with sugar on my first night and was hooked.

Cynthia and I went and sat by the open window in the lounge. Mary approached us, carrying two cups of tea, and handed one to each of us. "Do you young ladies want lights, or do you enjoy the twilight?" she asked.

"Twilight is lovely," I replied. "I think it's a full moon tonight."

"Mary!" Emily called from the other room. "My tea?"

Mary sighed in frustration and mumbled, "She never asks Lawrence or John to bring her tea."

"I'll bring it to her," said Cynthia.

Alfred stood. "No, I will bring Emily her tea." He poured it out and went out of the room, carrying it carefully.

Lawrence followed him, and Mary sat next to Cynthia and me.

We three sat in silence, gazing at the stars and the moon shining over Lake Superior. It was a glorious night, with a mild, wet breeze.

"It's almost too warm," Mary murmured. "I think a thunderstorm is brewing."

A warm bubble of contentment expanded inside of me, but that bubble was rudely burst by the sound of a breathy voice that made my stomach turn. "Good evening, ladies." Dr. Blake had somehow silently slinked in, and now he loomed over us.

"Dr. Blake!" exclaimed Cynthia. "What a funny time to come."

Mary was unruffled. "Have a seat. We're gazing at the moon."

Dr. Doom did as she requested, and for a while, we watched for the northern lights, his heavy breathing the only sound in the room. Then Alfred came back after delivering Emily's tea.

"Oh good, you're alright," Alfred said to the doctor. To the rest of us, he said, "I looked through the office window and saw him fall. So, I called out and told him to come in and dry off."

Dr. Doom laughed self-consciously, as he described how he had discovered a very rare species of fern in an inaccessible place, and in his efforts to get it, he lost his footing and slipped into a nearby bog pond.

"My pants are muddy and damp, but otherwise, I'm fine."

Emily called for Cynthia from the lobby, and she shot up to see what Emily wanted.

"Just carry up my briefcase and my laptop, will you, dear? I'm going to bed."

The door into the lobby was a wide one. I stood when Cynthia did, and John was close by me. There were, therefore, three witnesses who could swear that Emily was carrying her tea, still untasted, in her hand.

After that, we all sat around, and I at least waited for Dr. Blake to leave. It felt like he would never leave. He rose at last, however, and I breathed a sigh of relief.

"I'll walk down to the village with you," said Alfred. "I need to see our agent over those estate accounts."

"At this time of night?" John asked.

Alfred nodded. "Don't wait up. I have my key."

THREE

THE NIGHT
OF THE TRAGEDY

In the middle of the night, Lawrence shook me awake. Light from the hallway streamed into my bedroom, and his pale face and huge, scared eyes told me that something was seriously wrong.

"What is it?" I asked, sitting up in bed, and trying to shake off my sleepiness.

"It's Emily. She sounds like she's having a fit, and she's locked herself in her room."

Instantly, I slipped into security guard mode. "Let's go." Luckily, I'd worn flannel pajama pants and a black T-shirt to bed, so I was decent. I sprang out of bed and followed Lawrence along the passage to the right wing of the lodge.

John joined us, and Dorcas stood there in a state of awe-stricken excitement. Lawrence turned to his brother.

"What do you think we should do?"

John's indecisiveness rattled me. He flushed and furrowed his brow but said nothing.

"We need to get into her room," I stated. "Who has a key?"

"Only Alfred," said John. "He took it with him when he went out this evening."

John rattled the handle of Emily's door violently, but it was no use, as the door was obviously locked or bolted on the inside. We could hear Emily's groans. We had to do something, fast.

"Go through Alfred's room," cried Dorcas. "Oh, poor Emily!"

That's when it hit me that Alfred wasn't around. Surely, he wasn't still out talking business in the middle of the night? John opened the door of Alfred's room. It was pitch dark, but Lawrence hit the light and we saw that the bed had not been slept in, and that there was no sign of Alfred anywhere.

I went straight to the connecting door and rattled it. "It's also locked from the inside!" My frustration rose, threatening to overtake me.

"Oh no!" cried Dorcas, wringing her hands, "What do we do?"

"Call 911," I said to Dorcas. "And while we wait for them to get here, we have to break the door in." I turned to John, who was the biggest and the strongest of us all. "Do you think you can kick it in? Or should we find an ax?"

"Wait," said John. "Isn't there another through Cynthia's room?"

"Yeah," replied Lawrence. "But it's always bolted. It's never been undone."

"Well, let's go see," I said.

We ran rapidly down the hall to Cynthia's room. Mary was already there, shaking Cynthia, who must have been an unusually sound sleeper, and trying to wake her.

I tried the adjoining door. "No good. It's bolted too. But I think it's less solid than the others, so let's try to break this one in."

We strained and heaved together. The framework of the door was solid, and for a long time it resisted our efforts, but at last it gave way beneath our weight, and finally, with a resounding crash, it burst open.

We stumbled in together, Lawrence first. Emily lay on the bed, consumed by violent convulsions. Her nightstand was overturned. As we entered, however, her limbs relaxed, and she fell back upon the pillows.

John went to the only mother he'd ever known while I unbolted the door that led to the hallway. I turned to Lawrence, thinking I should get out of the way now that they were in Emily's room, but the words froze on my lips. Lawrence was as white as chalk, and he was shaking. His eyes, petrified with terror, stared at something on the wall. It was like he saw something that turned him to stone. I instinctively followed the direction of his eyes, but I didn't see anything unusual.

Emily was now able to speak in short gasps. "Better now—very sudden—stupid of me—to lock myself in."

A shadow fell on the bed. Mary stood near the door with her arm around Cynthia, who trembled, and her eyes were glassy.

"Poor Cynthia is really freaked out," said Mary, in a low, clear voice.

I noticed a faint streak of daylight peeking through the window curtains. When I glanced at the clock (which was on the floor, since the nightstand was overturned) it read 5 a.m. And here I thought it was the middle of the night.

I was startled by a strangled cry from the bed. Fresh pain seized Emily, and she went into convulsions. I knew from my first aid training to ease her onto her side and clear her airway, but there wasn't anything else I could do. We were all powerless to help. A final convulsion lifted Emily from the bed, until she appeared to rest upon her head and her heels, with her body arched like that girl in *The Exorcist*. Mary whimpered and hid her face against John. The moments flew. Again, Emily arched like a contortionist.

At that moment, Dr. Blake, with an air of authority, pushed his way into the room. He stopped dead, staring at Emily, and, at the same instant, she cried out in a strangled voice, her eyes fixed on the doctor.

"Alfred—Alfred—" Then she fell back motionless on the pillows.

In one stride, the doctor reached the bed, and seizing her arms, worked them energetically, and then he tried artificial respiration. We watched him, fascinated, though I think we all knew in our hearts that it was too late, that nothing could be done.

Finally, he stopped, shaking his head gravely. At that moment, we heard a commotion outside. The ambulance had arrived. Dorcas ran down and showed the paramedics up to where Emily lay.

After they confirmed that Emily was dead, they put her on a stretcher and prepared to move her downstairs and out to the ambulance. One of the paramedics asked what happened.

Dr. Blake spoke instantly.

"I'm a doctor," he said, with a tinge of self-importance. "I was out for an early walk and heard the commotion. So, I ran up and tried to help ..." His hand rose as if it was separate from his body, and he indicated the figure on the bed. "The convulsions were strangely violent. They were almost tetanic in character."

The paramedic cocked his head in question.

"Can we speak in private?" said Dr. Blake. He turned to John. "You don't mind?"

John, obviously in shock, simply shrugged. We all trooped out into the hall, leaving the two medical professionals alone, and I heard the key turned in the lock behind us.

We went slowly down the stairs. My heart was beating so fast, I thought it might burst through my chest. Every instinct told me that Dr. Blake had something to hide.

Mary placed her hand on my shoulder. "What is it, Helen? What are you thinking?"

I looked at her. "Listen!" I looked around, making sure the others were out of earshot. I lowered my voice to a whisper. "I think Dr. Blake suspects foul play. He was implying that Emily was poisoned."

"*What?*" Mary shrank against the wall, the pupils of her eyes dilating wildly. Then, suddenly, she cried out: "No, no—not that— not that!" She bolted upstairs, and I followed her, afraid that she was going to faint. I found her leaning against the wall, deadly pale. She waved me away impatiently.

"Go away, Helen. I want to be alone."

Reluctantly, I obeyed. John and Lawrence were in the dining room, so I joined them. We were all silent, but I suppose I voiced the thoughts of us all when I asked, "Where is Alfred?"

John shook his head. "He's not in the lodge."

Our eyes met. Where *was* Alfred? Emily's last words were his name. What would she have said about him if she'd had more time?

At last Dr. Blake and the paramedic came downstairs. Dr. Blake, in an odd blend of gloom and barely contained excitement, spoke to John. "They're obviously going to perform an autopsy."

"Why do you say 'obviously'?" asked John gravely. A spasm of pain crossed his face.

"Because the cause of death is unclear."

John bent his head. "I understand."

The paramedic betrayed no emotion. "We'll perform the autopsy as soon as possible, but in the meantime, you should call the police. If you don't, they'll be called in anyway, soon enough."

John nodded his ascent, and the paramedic walked out. After a moment, we heard the abrupt squeal of the ambulance starting up, but it quickly went silent and drove desolately away. There was no need for sirens, no reason for it to arrive quickly to its destination.

A heavy silence hung in the room. John broke it by asking Dr. Blake, "Is it really necessary to call in the police? We're all grieving right now. I'd rather not have the police involved."

An idea popped into my head. But I wasn't sure how John would respond. As a politician, he hated bad publicity; he was an easygoing optimist who shied away from conflict. But Lawrence was less conventional, a novelist who could perhaps appreciate the imagination in my idea. Maybe he could be an ally.

Either way, someone had to take charge, and since I was often the calm in the center of a storm, I decided to step in.

"John," I said, "You know my friend Perle, who Cynthia invited to stay here? She is an incredible detective."

John furrowed his brow in question.

"Let's have her investigate," I said.

"What—now?!"

"Yes, time is an advantage if—if—there has been foul play."

"Bullshit!" cried Lawrence angrily. He spoke directly to Dr. Blake, who cowered in the corner of the room. "Poisons are your obsession, so you invented some conspiracy and convinced the paramedic that Emily was murdered. If it wasn't for you, we could mourn our mother in peace."

Wow. Lawrence's heated attitude threw me for a loop. It was the first time I saw him get worked up about anything.

John raised his hand, palm out. "Stop, Lawrence. Dr. Blake was trying to help." He spoke to me. "Helen, can Perle be discrete? We don't want any unnecessary scandal."

"Of course," I cried eagerly, "she's the epitome of discretion."

"Fine, as long as she doesn't post about it on her blog or on social media, I give you free reign."

I looked at my watch. It was six o'clock. Perle once mentioned she was an early riser, and besides, surely the commotion with the ambulance woke her.

I stood. "Come on, Cynthia. I need you to show me the condo where Perle is staying."

PERLE INVESTIGATES

Cynthia led me down a narrow path through a thicket of trees, which cut off the detours of the winding drive. "They're that way," she said, pointing toward a set of buildings which must be condos. "Perle is in number two."

Cynthia turned then, and I said, "Wait. You're not coming with me?"

She shook her head. "I don't feel well."

I didn't doubt it. The image of Emily convulsing was burnt in my mind, and the sound of her crying for Alfred still rang in my ears. It was enough to make me nauseous, and I wasn't close to Emily like Cynthia had been. "Okay," I said. "Thanks for showing me the way."

I was nearly to condo #2, when I was startled by Alfred running toward me.

He came right up into my personal space, and for a second, I thought he was about to hit me.

"My God! This is terrible! My poor wife! I only just heard."

"Where have you been?" I asked.

"Denby kept me late last night. It was one o'clock before we'd finished. We'd had a few beers, so I crashed on his couch."

This aging hipster was fifty? He sounded like a dude in his mid-twenties. "How did you hear the news?" I asked.

"John called me on my cell. My poor Emily! She was selfless, and I guess she pushed herself too hard."

I experienced a wave of revulsion. He was such a hypocrite!

"I better hurry," I said. Thankfully, he didn't ask me where I was going.

In a few moments, I was knocking on Perle's door. There was no answer, so I knocked again, rather impatiently. A window above me cautiously opened, and Perle looked out.

"Helen? What is the matter?"

In a few brief words, I explained the morning's tragedy, and that we needed her help.

"Hold on, I will let you in, and you will tell me everything while I get dressed."

Hmm. I still wore my flannel pajama pants and T-shirt, though I'd thrown on Crocs and a hoodie before I went outside. Perle would definitely not approve, but there was nothing to do about it now.

In a few moments, Perle opened the front door, and I followed her up to her room. "Please, have a seat, and tell me exactly what happened."

I related the whole story, holding nothing back, leaving out no detail, however insignificant, while Perle got dressed in a pair of pressed, dark denim jeans, a crewneck cashmere sweater, and a silk scarf tied around her neck. She piled her hair into a bun on top of her head and applied just enough makeup to even her skin tone and brighten her eyes.

I told her how Douglas woke me, of Emily's dying words, of her husband's absence, of the argument the day before, of the conversation between Mary and her mother-in-law that I had overheard, and even of the falling out between Emily and Evie, and Evie's warnings before she left.

I was exhausted, muddled, and probably still in shock, so I'm sure I made a mess while recounting everything. I repeated myself several times, and once or twice had to go back to some detail that I had forgotten. Perle's smile was forgiving.

"The mind is confused? Is it not so? Take time, *mon ami*. You are agitated; you are excited—it is but natural. When you feel calmer, we will neatly arrange the facts, each in its proper place. We will examine—and reject. Those of importance we will put on one side; those of no importance, pouf!"—she screwed up her cherub-like face, and puffed comically enough—"blow them away!"

"Well sure," I conceded, "but how do you decide what is important, and what isn't? That's the difficult part."

Perle shook her head energetically. Then, she went back to arranging her bun with exquisite care.

"Not so. One fact leads to another—so we continue. Does the next fit in with that? Good! We can proceed. This next little fact—no! There is something missing—a link in the chain that is not there. We examine. We search. And that little detail that will not fit, we put it here!" She made an extravagant gesture with her hand. "It is significant! It is tremendous!"

"Y—es——"

"Ah!" Perle shook her forefinger so fiercely that I shrank before it. "Beware! Danger to the detective who says: 'It is so small—it does not matter. Forget about it.' That way lies confusion! Everything matters."

"I know. You always told me that. That's why I described all the details whether they seemed relevant or not."

"And I am pleased with you. You have a good memory, and you have given me the facts faithfully. But the order you presented them in ..." She narrowed her eyes, "... that was not okay! But I forgive you because you are upset. Even though you left out one fact of supreme importance."

"And what was that?" I asked.

"You didn't tell me if Emily ate well last night."

I stared at her. Surely her ballerina bun was too tight and was thus affecting her brain. Now she carefully brushed lint from her sweater, consumed by the task.

"I don't remember," I said. "And, anyway, I don't see——"

"You do not see? But it is so relevant."

"Okay." I took a deep breath and resisted rolling my eyes. "I don't believe she ate much. She was obviously upset, and naturally had no appetite."

"Yes," said Perle thoughtfully, "it was only natural."

She straightened herself and from her chair, clutched a sleek black bag large enough to carry a laptop and phone. Then she turned to me.

"Now I am ready. We will go to the lodge, and study matters on the spot. Excuse me, *mon ami*, you dressed in haste, and your hoodie string is tangled. Permit me." With a deft gesture, she rearranged it. "Voila! Now, shall we start?"

We hurried up the property. Perle stopped for a moment, and gazed solemnly over the beautiful expanse of beach, still glittering with morning dew.

"It's such beautiful surroundings, and yet, the poor family, plunged in sorrow and overwhelmed with grief."

She looked at me keenly as she spoke, and I was aware that I reddened under her prolonged gaze.

Was the sorrow at Emily's death overwhelming? It occurred to me how unmoved Emily's family seemed. She didn't command a lot of love. Her death was a shock and a distress, but nobody was distraught.

Perle seemed to follow my thoughts. She nodded her head gravely.

"No, you are right," she said, as if I'd voiced my thoughts, "there was no blood tie. She has been kind and generous to the Cavendish family, but she was not their own mother. Blood tells—always remember that—blood tells."

"Perle," I said, "why did you want to know if Emily ate well last night? I don't understand what it has to do with anything."

She was silent for a minute or two as we walked along, but finally she said, "I do not mind telling you—though, as you know, it is my habit to not explain until the end. But I am inclined to believe that Emily died of strychnine poisoning, probably administered in her tea."

"Okay. And?"

"Well, what time was the tea served?"

"About eight o'clock."

"Therefore, she drank it between then and half-past eight—certainly not much later. Well, strychnine is a fairly rapid poison. Its effects would be felt very soon, probably in about an hour. Yet, in Emily's case, the symptoms do not manifest themselves until five o'clock the next morning, nine hours! But a heavy meal, taken at about the same time as the poison, might delay its effects, though hardly to that extent." Her fingers lightly passed over the back of her neck, an unconscious gesture made while deep in thought. "Still, it is a possibility. But, according to you, she ate very little for supper, and yet the symptoms didn't develop until early the next morning! Now that is strange, my friend. Something may arise at the autopsy to explain it. In the meantime, remember it."

As we neared the house, John came out and met us. His face was haggard and gray, like he'd aged ten years overnight. I introduced him to Perle.

"Thank you, Perle, for coming to our aid," he said. "Helen has explained that we don't want any publicity?"

"I completely understand."

He gave her an intense gaze. "You see, right now we have nothing but suspicion to go on."

"Precisely. It is a matter of precaution only."

Grave nods were exchanged. Then, Perle and I went up together to Emily's room.

Once up there, Perle set straight to work. First, she locked the door on the inside, and carefully inspected the room. She darted from one object to the other with the agility of a cat. I stood by the door, afraid of unintentionally tampering with the evidence. Perle wasn't impressed.

"My friend," she cried, "why are you acting like a stuck pig?"

"I don't want to compromise the evidence."

"Compromise the evidence? Come on! There's been an army in the room! No, get over here and help."

She examined the locked briefcase which held the papers Emily printed before bed last night, and at her laptop, which was password-protected. She also tried to unlock Emily's briefcase but was unsuccessful. "Later," Perle muttered. Next, she examined the framework of the door we had broken in. Then she went to the door opposite leading into Cynthia's room. That door was also bolted, as I had stated. However, she unbolted it, opening and shutting it several times; this she did with great care and without making any noise. Suddenly something in the bolt seemed to rivet her attention. She examined it carefully, and then, nimbly whipping out a pair of small forceps from her bag, she drew out some minute particle, which she carefully sealed up in a tiny envelope.

On the dresser was a Keurig machine, and beside it, a nearly empty cup. How could I have missed such a detail? It was a clue worth having. Perle delicately dipped her finger into liquid, tasted it gingerly, and grimaced.

"Cocoa—with—I think—rum in it."

She passed on to the debris on the floor, where the nightstand was overturned. A reading-lamp, some books, matches, a bunch of keys, and the crushed fragments of a teacup were scattered about.

"Odd," said Perle.

"What's odd?"

"The lamp that fell from the nightstand is a little bent up. But the teacup is smashed to powder."

"So … someone stepped on the teacup?"

"Exactly," said Perle, in a near hiss. "Someone stepped on it and crushed it. Obviously using force."

She walked slowly across to the mantelpiece, where, deep in thought, she fiddled with the framed photos and glass bird figurines and straightened them—a sign she was agitated.

"*Mon ami*," she said, turning to me, "somebody stepped on that cup, grinding it to powder, and it was either because it contained strychnine or—which is far more serious—because it did not contain strychnine!"

I knew better than to respond. Yes, I was so confused that I felt a headache coming on, but there was no point asking Perle to explain.

A moment later, she shook off her deep thoughts and continued investigating. She reopened the laptop and tried to log on, typing various passwords. None of her guesses were correct, however.

"We must find a way to log on as soon as possible!"

Then she carefully examined the rest of the room. Crossing to the left-hand window, a round stain, hardly visible on the dark brown carpet, interested her deeply.

She got down on her knees, examining—even smelling it.

Finally, she poured a few drops of the cocoa into a test tube she inexplicably had in her bag, sealing it up carefully.

She took her phone and ejected a stylus from its base and began writing on it like it was a notepad. "We have found in this room," she said, writing busily, "six points of interest. Shall I list them, or will you?"

"Oh, definitely you," I quickly replied.

"Alright, then. One, a coffee-cup that has been ground into powder; two, a password protected laptop and a locked briefcase; three, a stain on the floor."

"That may have happened a while ago," I interrupted.

"No. It is still damp and smells like tea. Four, a fragment of some dark green fabric—only a thread or two, but recognizable."

"Oh!" I cried. "That's what you sealed up in the envelope."

"Yes. It may turn out to be from Emily's clothing, and unimportant. We shall see. Five, *this!*" With a dramatic gesture, she pointed to the floor, where there was a splash of wax from a scented candle. "It must be recent, otherwise Emily would have had it removed with parchment paper and a hot iron. One of my best scarves once—but that is beside the point."

"Maybe Emily knocked over the candle."

"Hmm …" Perle looked around the room. "Was it burning when you entered the room last night?"

Another detail I did not remember. "I don't know. But I remember Lawrence saw something on the mantle that seemed to paralyze him."

"Interesting," Perle said quickly.

"Why? What do you think?"

Perle only made a rather irritating reply, urging me to figure it out on my own.

"And the sixth point?" I asked. "Is it the cocoa?"

"No," said Perle thoughtfully. "I might have included that in the six, but no. For now, I am keeping the sixth point to myself."

She looked quickly round the room. "There is nothing more to be done here, I think, unless"—she stared earnestly and long at the dead ashes in the grate. "An actual wood-burning fireplace. I suppose it's part of the lodge's charm."

"The fireplace in my room is gas," I stated. "I suppose they can't take a chance in the guest rooms, but for Emily's own room, she made an exception.

"Yes," replied Perle. "The fire burns—and it destroys. But by chance—there might be—let us see!"

Deftly, on hands and knees, she began to sort the ashes from the grate into the fender, handling them with the greatest caution. Suddenly, she gave a faint exclamation.

"The tweezers, Helen!"

I quickly handed them to her, and with skill, she extracted a small piece of half-charred paper.

"There, *mon ami!*" he cried. "What do you think of that?"

I scrutinized the fragment. This is an exact reproduction of it:

ll and te

I was puzzled. What could Perle possibly see? But then it hit me.

"Perle!" I cried. "This is a fragment of a will!"

"Exactly."

I looked at her sharply.

"You are not surprised?"

"No." Her voice was low, her face like stone. "I expected it."

My brain was in a whirl. If this was a will, who had destroyed it? The person who knocked over the candle? Obviously. But how did that person get in? All the doors had been bolted on the inside.

"Now, my friend," said Perle briskly, "we will go. I want to interview the maid—Dorcas, right?"

We passed through Alfred's room, and quickly examined it. We went out through that door, locking both it and Emily's room as before.

I took her down to the office and went to find Dorcas. When I returned with her, I found Perle examining the wall-sized shelves, which were artistically organized with brown, orange, and white boxes and binders, all labeled and strategically placed.

"Admirable!" she murmured. "Admirable! What symmetry! Observe the placement—neatness rejoices the eye. The spacing is perfect. It was recently done; correct?"

"Yes, I believe Emily worked on it yesterday afternoon. But— Dorcas is here."

"Helen, do not begrudge me a moment's satisfaction of the eye."

"Yes, but this is important."

"And how do you know that this beautiful filing system is not of equal importance?"

I shrugged. There was really no arguing with her.

Perle turned and addressed Dorcas. "Please, have a seat."

"Thank you." Dorcas looked like she wanted to be anywhere but here, but she sat in an overstuffed armchair.

Perle remained standing "How long did you work for Emily?"

"Ten years."

"That is a long, faithful service. You were very loyal, yes?"

"She was a good boss."

Perle's fingers absently brushed the back of her neck. "Then you don't mind answering a few questions?"

Dorcas gave a brief nod, indicating half-hearted consent.

"Tell me about yesterday afternoon. Emily had an argument?"

"Yes. But I don't think I should——" Dorcas hesitated.

Perle sat across from her, so they were on eye level with each other. "Dorcas, I need to know every detail. You aren't betraying Emily's secrets. Emily is dead, and if we're going to avenge her, we need to know what happened in the hours before her death. Nothing can bring her back to life, but we do hope, if there has been foul play, to bring the murderer to justice."

"Amen to that," said Dorcas fiercely.

"Now, when did you hear her arguing?"

Dorcas hesitated, but then clearly resigned herself to share what she knew. "I happened to be going along the hall outside yesterday—"

"What time was that?"

"Maybe four o'clock? I passed by the office and heard Emily … she sounded upset. I didn't mean to eavesdrop, but …"

"But what did you hear?" Pearle leaned in, suddenly intense.

Dorcas's chest heaved. Emily said, "'You have lied, and deceived me.' I didn't hear what Alfred said back. He spoke a good bit lower than she did—but she answered, 'How dare you? You owe me everything!' Again, I didn't hear what he said, but she went on. 'Nothing that you can say will make any difference. My mind is made up.' Then I thought I heard them coming, so I walked away."

"You are sure it was Alfred's voice you heard?"

"Yes. I mean, who else could it be?"

"Well, what happened next?"

Dorcas pressed her lips together, inhaling through her nose. "Later, I went to check on Emily. She looked pale and upset. 'Dorcas,' she said, 'I think I'm in shock.' I told her I was sorry to hear it, and she'd feel better after a nice hot cup of tea. She had something in her hand. I don't know if it was a letter, or just a piece of paper, but it had writing on it, and she kept staring at it, almost as if she couldn't believe what was written there. She whispered to herself, as though she had forgotten I was there: 'These few words—and everything's changed.' And then she said, 'Never trust a man, Dorcas, they're not worth it!' I got her a cup of tea, and she thanked me. Then Mary came in."

"Emily still had the letter, or whatever it was, in her hand?"

"Yes."

Perle leaned back and crossed her legs. "Now, to change the subject, did Emily have any dark green clothing?"

Dorcas wrinkled her face in confusion. "No."

"Are you sure?"

"Yes. Emily preferred warm colors, like red and pink."

"Good, we will move on. Do you know if Emily took a sleeping pill last night?"

"Not *last* night. I know she didn't."

"How are you so sure?"

"Because the bottle was empty. She had this sleep powder, and she used the last of it two days ago, and she didn't refill the prescription."

"Thank you, Dorcas, that is all I have to ask you."

"I can go?" asked Dorcas.

Perle nodded. After Dorcas left, I asked, "How did you know that Emily took something to sleep?"

"I knew because of this." She suddenly, seemingly out of nowhere, produced an empty prescription bottle.

"Where did you find it?"

"In the drawer of Emily's overturned nightstand. It was Number Six of my catalog."

"But if she used the last of it two days ago, it wouldn't be important."

"Probably not but look at the label."

I examined it closely, and then looked at Perle in question.

She raised her eyebrows and repeated herself like I just hadn't heard her. "Look at the label."

"I did. I don't see anything unusual."

Perle shook her head in disapproval. "Where is the name of the doctor who prescribed it?"

I reexamined the bottle. "Oh!" I exclaimed. "There isn't one. That is strange!"

I was getting worked up, but Perle said, "The explanation is simple. I will tell you later." She patted me on the shoulder. If she had been tall enough, she probably would have patted me on the head.

Perle scanned the room and pointed to the smaller desk in the corner. "Whose desk is that?"

"I think it's Alfred's."

"Ah!" She sat at his desk and pressed on the computer's keyboard, making the screen come to life. "Locked. But perhaps I can guess his password." She typed something quickly, and immediately unlocked the computer. "*Voilà!*" Perle gave me a satisfied grin. "Helen, don't ever use 'password123' unless you wish to be hacked."

"Don't worry, I won't."

She clicked on files, opening them. "Alfred Inglethorp is a man of method!"

A "man of method" was, in Perle's estimation, the highest praise possible. How could she be so complimentary, especially after his super lame password?

It wouldn't be the last time I'd wonder if I had made a mistake, involving Perle in this mess.

FIVE

NEVER CHOOSE POPPYSEED

"Come," she said, "now to examine the teacups!"

"But why? Emily clearly drank the cocoa long after she drank the tea."

"Ugh. That miserable cocoa!" cried Perle flippantly.

She laughed, raising her arms to heaven in mock despair, and I was shocked she would joke about murder and poison.

"Fine." My voice had a cold edge. "But Emily took her tea upstairs with her, so I don't know what you expect to find. Do you think there's a packet of strychnine on the tea tray?!"

Perle sobered at once. "Come on, Helen." She slipped her arm through mine. "Indulge my interest in the teacups, and I will respect your cocoa. There! Is it a bargain?"

She was so earnest and elfin that I had to laugh; and we went together to the lobby, where the teacups and tray remained undisturbed as we had left them.

"Helen, please describe what happened the night before with

the tea. Provide every detail."

I did my best, and she listened carefully, nodding her head. "So, Mary stood by the tray—and the tea. Then crossed to the window and sat with you and Cynthia. Yes. Here are the three cups. And the cup on the mantelpiece, half drunk, that would belong to Lawrence. And the one on the tray?"

"I saw John put it there."

"Good. One, two, three, four, five—but where, then, where was Alfred's cup?"

"He doesn't like tea."

"Then all are accounted for. One moment, my friend."

She sniffed and examined each cup carefully. "Excellent!" she said at last. "It is clear! I had an idea—but I was mistaken. Yes, altogether I was mistaken. Yet it is strange. But never mind!"

I could have told her that the tea obsession was a dead end, but I held my tongue.

"Breakfast is ready," said John, coming in from the hall. "It's nothing much, just coffee and bagels, but I thought it was important that we eat. Perle, will you join us?"

"Yes, thank you," she replied.

John had changed into a clean flannel shirt (the stylish kind from Prana) and a pair of khaki pants. His face was no longer gray, and his hair was combed. In fact, he seemed nearly back to his normal self. Sure, last night's events threw him, but he had rebounded quickly. It occurred to me that as competent as he was, his imagination was limited. Mary had been right about that. Meanwhile, Lawrence had an overactive imagination. John was the practical older sibling. All morning he'd made phone calls (including one to Evie), sent emails, and contacted the press. Because that's what you do when someone dies and you're in the public eye.

John cleared his throat. "Can I ask if you've found anything yet?

Do you think she died a natural death, or should we steel ourselves for the worst?"

"It's too soon to say," said Perle. "What does the rest of your family believe happened?"

"Lawrence thinks we're being dramatic and that Emily just had heart failure."

"He does, does he? That is very interesting—very interesting," murmured Perle softly. "And your wife?"

A faint cloud passed over John's face. "I have no idea what she thinks."

Talk about an awkward moment. John broke the uncomfortable silence by saying, "I told you, didn't I, that Alfred is back?"

Perle nodded.

"It's horrific," John continued. "We have to act normal around him, but I'm about to eat bagels with the guy who murdered my mother."

Perle placed her hand on his shoulder. "I understand. Shall we go eat?"

"I'll meet you there," I said. "I want to change clothes and freshen up first."

Perle breathed a sigh of relief. "Yes, Helen. I am glad you realize that is necessary. We will see you in the dining room."

I went upstairs, and quickly washed up, splashing water on my face and underneath my arms. I put on deodorant, combed my hair, and pulled it back into a neat ponytail. I even applied a bit of mascara and lip gloss. Then I changed into a pale blue Oxford shirt and black leggings. Perle probably wouldn't approve, but it was the best I could do.

By the time I got downstairs, everyone was in the dining room, pouring themselves coffee and spreading cream cheese onto bagels. Of course, the mood was somber, as we all still suffered from shock. But our Minnesota Nice was also on full display, so nobody acted out. Yet, there were no red eyes, no clear attempts to contain wild grief. If anyone was in deep mourning, it was Dorcas.

Alfred sat, eating a bagel, unaware of the dab of pink cream cheese on the left side of his mouth. Would I have been so revolted had anyone else needed to wipe their mouth? Probably not. He seemed unafraid and had no sense of the collective suspicion pressing him down. Either he was a dense but innocent man, or he was guilty and completely arrogant, believing his crime would go unpunished.

I stood at the buffet, selected a poppy seed bagel, spread it with maple walnut cream cheese, and poured myself some coffee. Then I sat next to Perle. She interrupted her conversation to whisper in my ear, "*Mon amie*, Helen, never choose a poppy seed bagel. The little black seeds are sure to lodge between your teeth."

"Excuse," I said to those around me. "I've changed my mind. I think I'll have a plain bagel instead."

I got up and prepared a new bagel, observing the interactions of everyone in the room as I did so.

Mary sat at the head of the table, graceful, composed, enigmatic. In her soft gray sweater, she looked almost as put together as Perle. She was silent, hardly opening her lips even as she ate and drank. Yet her strength of personality somehow dominated the room.

Cynthia seemed tired and ill, with heavy and slow movements. I sat back down between her and Perle, and said, "Are you okay, Cynthia?"

Perle overheard and said, "You poor dear. Let me get you another cup of coffee. It's great for headaches." Perle retrieved her cup and poured.

"No sugar," said Cynthia, watching her as she picked up the sugar-tongs.

"No sugar?"

"I never take it in coffee."

"That's right," I said. "You don't like it in tea either, even though it helps absorb the catechins."

Perle murmured something to herself, as she brought back the replenished cup.

Only I heard her, and I saw that her face worked with suppressed excitement, and her eyes were as green as a cat's.

"What is it?" I whispered.

Perle's nostrils flared, ever so slightly. She whispered back. "You should have told me that Cynthia doesn't like sugar in her tea."

My mouth dropped open, yet no response came out. Perle turned away from me and spoke to John, who sat across from her. "If it is too soon to ask some questions about Emily's will, please let me know. But any information you might give, will help."

"I'm happy to answer your questions," said John.

"Alright," said Perle. "I hope I do not violate etiquette, but in the event of Emily's death, who inherits her money?"

All eyes were on John. He paused, and then softly replied. "By her last will, dated August of last year, other than some small gifts to employees, she gave everything to me."

If this shocked Perle, she did not let on. "I see." Her gaze wandered from John, to Lawrence, to Alfred, and then back to John.

"Was not that—pardon the question—rather unfair to Lawrence?"

Lawrence grunted out a laugh. He and John glared at each other.

"No," John replied, "I have put a lot of my time and money into the Styles Resort. Emily left me her money so I can continue with its upkeep."

Perle nodded thoughtfully.

"When Emily remarried, did she plan to change her will?" She glanced at Alfred, but his lips stayed pressed shut.

"She was going to," said John unexpectedly. "We discussed her will only yesterday."

"You need to say the rest of it," Lawrence interjected angrily. He leaned in, making eye contact with Perle. "Emily changed her will all the time, like, once a year. Sometimes she'd leave it all to John, or to me, or divide it between us, or then she'd change it again and leave her money to someone outside of the family, like Evie."

"Do you know if she could have recently changed her will?" Perle asked.

"No," admitted John. "She was vague when we spoke yesterday. I don't know when she last changed it."

"There *is* a later will." It was Perle who spoke.

"What?" John raised his eyebrows, startled.

"Yes. See here." She took out the charred fragment we had found in the grate in Emily's room. Perle explained what it was and where we found it.

"But possibly this is an old will?" Lawrence asked.

"I do not think so," said Perle. "She printed documents last night, yes? I believe she printed this most recent version of her will, and then it wound up burned."

"Well, that's an awful coincidence," John cleared his throat and remarked drily, "that Emily would change her will only hours before she died."

"Are you so sure it is a coincidence?" Perle asked.

"What do you mean?"

"Your mother, you tell me, had a heated argument with—someone yesterday afternoon—"

"What do you mean?" cried John again. There was a tremor in his voice, and he had gone very pale.

Perle patiently continued. "Afterward, your mother very suddenly and hurriedly makes a new will. We don't know what it says. If we can't access her laptop, then she takes its secret with her to her grave."

At that moment, there was a call from the lobby. "John? Mary? Hello! I'm back."

"Evie!" John bolted up.

"Ah, I am glad she has come," Perle remarked.

I followed John and went out into the hall to greet Evie. As her eyes fell on me, I experienced a sudden pang of guilt. This was the woman who had warned me so earnestly, and I'd ignored her. Now she was tragically justified, and shame burned my cheeks. If she'd stayed at Styles, would Emily still be alive? Perhaps Alfred would have felt her watchful eye and held back.

Evie shook my hand with a strong, painful grip. Her sad eyes met mine, but I sensed no blame, only that she had been crying bitterly; I could tell by the redness of her eyelids.

"I got here as soon as I could," said Evie.

"Have you eaten anything this morning, Evie?" asked John.

"No."

"I didn't think so." He turned to me. "Look after her, Helen. Okay? I have more phone calls to make." He left without giving me a chance to answer, and at that moment, Perle came into the lobby.

"Evie, this is Perle. She's helping us."

Evie gave me a suspicious look. "What do you mean—helping us?"

"Helping us to investigate."

Evie huffed. "There's nothing to investigate." She spoke to Perle. "Have they taken him to prison yet?"

"Taken who to prison?" Perle asked.

"Who? My cousin, Alfred Inglethorp!"

"Be careful, Evie," I said. "Lawrence thinks Emily died of a heart attack."

"Lawrence is a fool!" she retorted. "Alfred obviously murdered poor Emily—I always told you he would. Anyone with any sense can see that he poisoned her. I always said he'd murder her in her bed and now he's done it."

Perle stayed silent, merely observing Evie's rant. I asked, "Well, what do you want us to do?"

Evie placed her hands on her hips. "Figure out how he did it! Did he lace her food, her Ibuprofen, her tea? Once you know his methods, then you can place the blame on him."

Something heavy trembled inside my stomach. How would Alfred and Evie live under the same roof? There might be more than one murder at Styles before the sun had set. "Come on," I said. "Let's get you something to eat."

Luckily, everyone else was clearing out. After Evie sat down with a bagel, Perle joined her. "I want to ask you something."

"Ask away," said Evie, giving Perle the evil eye.

"I want to count on your help."

Evie smirked. "That wasn't a question. However, I'll do whatever I can to help you prove that Alfred is guilty. He should hang for what he did."

"We are on the same page," said Perle. "More or less. I too, would like the criminal to be punished."

"Alfred," Evie stated flatly.

Perle tilted her head to the side. "Him, or someone else."

"Hmpf. Emily wasn't murdered until *he* came along. Lots of people were after her money, but her life was safe enough. Then along comes Alfred—and within two months—hey presto!"

"Believe me, Evie," said Perle very earnestly, "if Alfred is the man, he won't escape me. But I ask for your trust. Your help is very valuable, and I'll tell you why." Perle took a deep breath. "In this house, your eyes are the only that have shed any tears."

Evie blinked, and she choked up. "You know, Emily was selfish in her way. She was very generous, but she always wanted something in return. She never let people forget what she did for them—and, that way she missed love. She never realized it, though, or felt the lack of it. But I was on a different footing. I took my stand from the first, and I wouldn't accept any handouts. I kept my self-respect, and I was the only one who grew close to her. I protected her from all of them. Then Alfred comes along, and poof! All my years of devotion were for nothing."

Perle nodded sympathetically. "I understand how you feel. It is natural. You think that we are lukewarm—that we lack fire and energy—but trust me, it is not so."

John stuck his head in at that moment. "I looked through her files, and I think I found the password to Emily's computer. Should we give it a try?"

Perle nearly jumped from her chair. "Yes! Come, Helen. Let's go see."

On our way upstairs, John looked back to the dining-room door and lowered his voice confidentially. "What will happen when Aflred and Evie are in the same room together?"

I shook my head helplessly.

"I asked Mary to keep them apart if she can."

"Will she be able to?"

"Who knows. I'm banking on Alfred keeping his distance from Evie."

"You've got the keys still, haven't you, Perle?" I asked, as we reached the door of the locked room.

Taking the keys from Perle, John unlocked it, and we all entered.

John took her laptop from the dresser, where Perle left it. "Emily kept all her important documents on this." He opened it with one hand, and with the other hand, held the slip of paper with her password. When he tapped the computer to life, John gasped.

"What is it?" I asked.

"Someone already bypassed the lock screen. Her desktop popped right up."

"But that's impossible," cried Perle. "I could not get in this morning, not without a password."

"See." John showed her the opened desktop.

"No!" cried Perle, dumbfounded. "Her computer was hacked. I thought it would be safe, in this locked room. And I had both the keys in my pocket!" She flung the keys down.

"But who hacked it? When? Wasn't the door locked?" These questions burst from John and me disjointedly.

Perle went to the laptop and clicked a few times. "There are no files on this computer. It has been wiped clean, and the trash bin was permanently emptied."

"Maybe it can be recovered somehow," John said. "Lawrence is good with computers. I'll ask him."

John walked off with the computer, and to my surprise, Perle didn't seem to care. She was almost in a trance, and I watched her, fearing she might snap. Then, from the corner of my eye, I saw Emily's briefcase, lying abandoned on the floor. Someone had opened it. Inadvertently, I gasped. "What is it?" Perle demanded.

I didn't need to answer, because Perle followed my gaze. She went to the briefcase, held it up, and visibly sagged. "It's completely empty," she told me. "That's even worse than the laptop."

We stared at each other blankly. Perle dropped the briefcase and walked over to the mantelpiece. She was outwardly calm, but I noticed her hands, which from the force of habit of mechanically straightening the trinkets on the mantelpiece, shook violently.

"It was like this," she said at last. "There was something—some piece of evidence, enough of a clue to connect the murderer with the crime. It was vital that it was destroyed before it was discovered. Therefore, he took a risk, coming in here. It must have been something hugely important."

"But what was it?"

"Ah!" cried Perle, with a gesture of anger. "I don't know! A document of some kind, perhaps a new will? And now it is gone. It is destroyed. Perhaps there's a chance—we must leave no stone unturned—"

She rushed like a madwoman from the room, and I followed her a moment later. But, by the time I had reached the top of the stairs, she was out of sight.

Mary stood where the staircase branched, staring down into the hall in the direction in which she had disappeared.

"What happened, Helen? Perle just rushed past me like the house is on fire."

"She's upset about something," I remarked feebly. I didn't know how much Perle would want me to disclose. I decided to change the subject, and said, "They haven't run into each other yet, have they?"

"Who?"

"Alfred and Evie."

She gave such a level, steady gaze, that I caught my breath.

"Would that be such a disaster?"

"Umm, yeah. Don't you think it would be?"

"No." She smiled in her quiet way. "A confrontation would clear the air. Right now, we're all thinking too much, and not saying enough."

"John doesn't think so," I remarked. "He's anxious to keep them apart."

"Oh, John!"

Something in her tone bugged me, and I blurted out, "John is a good man."

She squinted, studying for a minute or two, and then said, "You are loyal to your friend. I like you for that."

"Aren't you my friend too?"

"I am a very bad friend."

"Why do you say that?"

"Because it is true. I am great to my friends one day and forget all about them the next."

I don't know what compelled me to reply, "You never seem to forget about Dr. Blake."

Instantly I regretted my words. Her face stiffened. I had the impression of a steel wall slamming down and removing her from view. Without a word, she turned and went swiftly up the stairs. I stood like an idiot gaping after her.

Yet, I was soon distracted by the sound of Perle shouting. I didn't think the entire lodge should hear her rant, so I stepped briskly down the stairs, hoping I could save us both from embarrassment. Seeing me, Perle calmed immediately. I pulled her aside.

"Perle, is it smart to share so much? You don't want to play into the criminal's hands."

"Is that right, Helen?"

"Yes."

She looked crestfallen, and part of me felt bad, while the other part believed I was smart to reprimand her.

"Well," she said at last, "let's go, *mon ami*."

"We're done here?"

"For now. You will walk me back to the condo?"

"Of course."

She picked up her bag, and we went out through the lobby. Cynthia was just coming in, and Perle stood aside to let her pass.

"Excuse me, Cynthia. One question"

"Yes?" she turned, raising her eyebrows. She at least seemed a bit more alert.

"Did you ever fill Emily's prescriptions?"

A slight flush rose in her face. "Only the ones that could also be bought over the counter."

"So the diphenhydramine hydrochloride?"

I furrowed my brow in question. "That's the active ingredient in Unisom," Perle explained to me.

Cynthia's blush increased. "It was a sleep powder whose main ingredients were magnesium, melatonin, and diphenhydramine hydrochloride. It's a rare blend and often out of stock. But it's not addictive."

"Ah! Thank you, Cynthia."

As we walked briskly away from the house, I glanced at her more than once. Perle's eyes shone like emeralds.

"Well, that explains the blank label on the pill bottle," I said. "I can't believe I didn't think of it."

Perle wasn't listening. "I discovered something in Emily's pristinely organized office. A file folder labeled 'wills.' The most recent was dated before her marriage, and it left her entire fortune to Alfred Inglethorp. It must have been made just at the time they were engaged. John Cavendish was surprised. It was written on one of those printed will forms and witnessed by two of the employees— not Dorcas."

"Did Alfred know about it?"

"He says he did not."

I sighed, hugging my chest in the cool morning air. "It's very confusing that she had so many wills." We reached the door to condo #2 and entered. "What do you think it means?"

"I believe that the most likely explanation is usually the correct one."

"So, Alfred is guilty," I said out loud, but I was talking more to myself than to Perle.

The room was airy and light, with high ceilings, a beige rug, and golden wood, just like in the lodge. Perle sat on the edge of the red velvet couch, not exactly reclining. She looked at me curiously.

"Are you sure of his guilt?"

"Of course." I sat across from her on a chair with carved wooden armrests. "It seems obvious to me."

Perle tilted her head to the side. "I don't know."

"Oh, come on!" I looked to the ceiling. "I can think of only one reason why it might not be him."

"What's that?"

I met her gaze. "He wasn't in the house last night."

"Oh, Helen." She frowned, yet her eyes smiled. "Think. If Alfred knew that his wife would be poisoned last night, of course he would have arranged to be out. His excuse was lame. So, either he knew what was going to happen or he had some other reason to be absent."

"Like what?"

Perle shrugged. "How should I know? Adultery, perhaps? Alfred is obviously a scoundrel. But that doesn't necessarily mean he's a murderer."

I shook my head, unconvinced.

"We do not agree?" Perle leaned back now and crossed her legs. "Well, time will show which of us is right. Now what do you make of all the doors of Emily's bedroom being bolted on the inside?"

"Well …" I considered it. "We should look at it logically."

"True."

"The doors *were* bolted; we saw that with our own eyes. But somehow, someone entered her room last night, otherwise you can't explain the spilled candle wax and the destroyed will. Do you agree?"

"Perfectly. Put with splendid lucidity. Proceed."

I straightened my posture, encouraged. "Whoever entered didn't climb through the window, nor did he use some magic force, so Emily must have let him in herself. That strengthens the conviction that it was Alfred. She would naturally open the door to her own husband."

Perle's near-smile turned to a scowl. "Think, Helen. Why would Emily let Alfred in? She bolted the door leading into his room, and she had a heated argument with him that afternoon. No, he was the last person she wanted to see."

"Hmm." Why hadn't I thought of that? Sure, I'd been married only briefly, but I still knew that after we fought, Paul was the last person I'd let into a room I had locked myself into.

Perle must have read my expression because she didn't press me. "Now, moving on. What do you think about what you overheard between Mary and Emily?"

"I forgot about that," I said thoughtfully. "It just seems unlike Mary, who is so elegant and reserved, to meddle in something that isn't her business."

"Precisely." Perle widened her eyes, like she was urging me to continue. But with a burst of guilt, I remembered what I said to Mary earlier about Dr. Blake, and I described the conversation to Perle, finishing with, "It's strange, but probably unimportant in the whole scheme of things."

A groan burst from Perle. "What have I always told you? Every detail is important. For example, Alfred's odd fashion sense, his waxed mustache, and his glasses—those things could be hugely important."

"Perle, you can't be serious."

"I am absolutely serious, my friend." She got up and laid her hand on my shoulder. Tears came to her eyes. "In all this, you see, I think of poor Emily, who is dead. She was not extravagantly loved, and she was an aging woman who fought invisibility. The world punishes women like Emily, ones who don't fade away into quiet acquiescence once they hit menopause. I'm not saying she was perfect, but she was a good person; she contributed a lot to her community, and she did not deserve to be killed."

I tried to interrupt, but Perle swept on.

"Let me tell you this, Helen. I would never forgive myself if I let Alfred Inglethorp, her husband, be arrested *now*—when a word from me could save him!"

S I X

THE INQUEST

There was an inquest. Neither Perle nor I had to testify, so we sat together.

Before the judge, John Cavendish described what happened on the morning that Emily died, giving all the details about the hot cocoa cup, the teacup, and the locked doors. After him, the doctor from Duluth who performed the autopsy, testified. He determined that Emily died from strychnine poisoning. He said that judging from the amount she took, and the fact that strychnine poisoning isn't exactly a household substance, the possibility that Emily took it by accident was next to zero.

Then, since Dr. Blake is both a poison expert and he had been there when Emily died, he testified next.

"Could the strychnine have been administered in Mrs. Inglethorp's after-dinner tea which was taken to her by her husband?"

"Possibly, but strychnine is a fairly rapid drug in its action. The symptoms usually appear a couple of hours after it has been swallowed. It is delayed under certain conditions, none of which, however, appear to have been present in this case. I know Emily

60

had the tea after dinner about eight o'clock, but the symptoms did not manifest until early the next morning, which, on the face of it, indicates that she took the drug much later in the evening."

The judge looked at some papers and asked, "Mrs. Inglethorp was in the habit of drinking a cup of cocoa in the middle of the night. Could the strychnine have been administered in that?"

"No, I took a sample of the cocoa remaining in the cup and had it analyzed. There was no strychnine."

I heard Perle chuckle softly beside me.

"How did you know?" I whispered.

"Listen."

"I should add," Dr. Blake continued, "that I would have been surprised at any other result."

"Why?"

"Because strychnine has an unusually bitter taste. It can only be disguised by a strongly flavored substance. Cocoa would never mask it."

The judge asked, "Would it be covered up by tea?"

"Possibly, depending on the tea. If it has a bitter taste of its own, it will probably cover the taste of strychnine."

"Then is it more likely that the drug was administered in the tea, but that the effect was delayed for an unknown reason?"

"Yes, but since the cup was completely smashed, there is no possibility of analyzing its contents."

That was it for Dr. Blake's evidence. Next, Emily's general physician, Dr. Wilkins corroborated it on all points. He also rejected the idea of suicide. The deceased, he said, suffered from a weak heart, but otherwise enjoyed perfect health, and displayed no signs of depression. She would be one of the last people to take her own life.

Lawrence Cavendish was called next. His evidence was mostly just a repeat of his brother's. Just as he was about to step down, he paused, and said, "Can I make a suggestion?"

He glanced deprecatingly at the judge. In clipped syllables, she responded, "Certainly, Mr. Cavendish, we are here to discover the truth. I welcome any pertinent information."

"It is just an idea," explained Lawrence. "Of course, I could be wrong, but I thought it might be a way to logically explain my mother's death."

"Go on, Mr. Cavendish."

"Well, I know she used a sleep powder that contained a small amount of the herb maqianzi, meant to treat arthritis pain. But if you take huge quantities, it can also cause strychnine poisoning."

In my peripheral vision, I saw Cynthia suck in a breath, and perhaps she went pale. It was hard to tell.

"Go on," said the judge.

"I went to medical school," continued Lawrence, "and I know that there have been cases where the cumulative effect of a drug, administered for some time, has caused death. Also, isn't it possible that she took an overdose of her medicine by accident?"

The judge shrugged. "I'm not a doctor, so I don't know."

At that, Dr. Wilkins spoke up, asking to take the stand again. "I'm afraid that idea is impossible," he said, once up there. "Any doctor would tell you the same. Strychnine is, in a certain sense, a cumulative poison, but it would be impossible for it to result in sudden death in this way. The amount of the herb maqianzi in her sleep powder was entirely safe. And there would have to be a long period of chronic symptoms which would at once have attracted my attention. The whole idea is crazy."

"And the second suggestion? That Mrs. Inglethorp may have overdosed?"

"Three, or even four doses, wouldn't result in death. Yes, her sleep powder had an herb that could mimic strychnine, but she would have had to take an obscene amount to explain all the strychnine found at the autopsy."

The judge focused her eagle eye on Dr. Wilkins. "So, can we accept that the sleep powder did not cause her death?"

"Yes. It's a ridiculous idea."

"What if the pharmacist who filled the prescription made a mistake?"

Dr. Wilkens had no good answer, but Dorcas, who was the next witness called, dispelled that possibility. The powder wasn't recently made up. In fact, Emily took the last dose on the day of her death.

The next witness was Mary Cavendish. She stood very upright, and spoke in a low, clear, and perfectly composed voice. In answer to the judge's question, she explained how she was startled by the sound of something heavy falling.

"That would have been the table by the bed?" asked the judge.

Mary nodded. "I opened my door," she continued, "and listened. Dorcas came running down and woke my husband, and we all went to my mother-in-law's room, but it was locked—"

The judge interrupted her. "You don't need to repeat what's already been attested to. But I'd like to know what you overheard from the argument the day before."

Mary raised her hand and adjusted the collar of her sweater, turning her head a little as she did so. And suddenly I thought, "She is buying time!"

"Is it true," continued the judge, "that you sat reading on the bench just outside the long window of the office?"

This was news to me, and glancing sideways at Perle, I assumed it was news to her as well.

A faint pause, a mere hesitation of a moment, and then she answered, "Yes, that is right."

"And the office window was open, was it not?"

I swear her face grew a little paler as she answered, "Yes."

"Then you heard the voices inside, especially since they were angry voices. In fact, they would be more audible where you were than in the lobby."

"Possibly."

"Will you repeat to us what you overheard of the argument?"

"I really do not remember hearing anything."

"So, you didn't hear voices?"

"Oh, yes, I heard voices, but I didn't hear exactly what they said." Faintly, her cheeks flushed. "I don't like to eavesdrop.

The judge persisted. "So, you remember nothing? *Nothing*, Mrs. Cavendish? Not one word or phrase that made you realize it *was* a private conversation?"

She paused, and seemed to reflect, still calm as ever.

"Yes; I remember. Emily said something—I do not remember exactly what—something about a scandal between husband and wife."

"I see!" The judge leant back. "That corresponds with what Dorcas heard. But excuse me, Mrs. Cavendish. You realized it was a private conversation, but you remained where you were?"

There was a gleam in her tawny eyes as she raised them. In that moment, she could have torn the judge and her insinuations into pieces, but she replied, "I was comfortable where I was. I simply wanted to read my book."

"Is that all you can tell us?"

"Yes."

Cynthia came next. She had, however, little to tell. She was unaware of the tragedy unfolding, until Mary woke her up.

"You did not hear the nightstand fall?"

"No. I was fast asleep."

The judge smiled. "A good conscience makes a sound sleeper," she observed. "Thank you, Miss Murdoch, that is all."

I whispered to Perle. "Should we say something about how Cynthia filled Emily's sleep powder prescription?"

Perle dismissed me with a wave of her hand.

The judge called the next witness. "Ms. Evie Howard."

Evie went up there and read the email that Emily wrote her shortly before her death. Perle and I had already seen it, so nothing new was added to our knowledge of the tragedy. The email read:

Evie,

Please, can we bury the hatchet? It's hard to forgive what you said about Alfred, but I trust you and don't want to lose our friendship.

All my best,

Emily

"*I* know her," Evie told the judge. "She wanted me back. But she wasn't going to admit that I was right."

Then came the most sensational testimony of the day. The judge called Albert Mace, a store clerk in Lutsen's only hardware store (as opposed to the one in Grand Marais, the slightly larger town a few miles away, where Cynthia worked.)

Albert seemed pale, though maybe he was naturally so. He explained that he had only recently started working at Lutsen Hardware.

The judge asked, "Mr. Mace, have you recently sold strychnine to any unauthorized person?"

"Yes, ma'am. The only strychnine we have available comes in a jar of Martin's Gopher Bait, and the customer must sign for it as they make the purchase."

"And when did you sell the gopher bait?"

"Last Monday night."

"Monday? Not Tuesday?"

"No, Monday, March 16th."

"Will you tell us to whom you sold it?"

You could have heard a pin drop.

"Yes, sir. It was to Mr. Inglethorp."

Every eye turned simultaneously to where Alfred Inglethorp sat, impassive and wooden. He started slightly, as the damning words fell from the young man's lips. I almost thought he would bolt from his chair, but he remained seated, with an Oscar-worthy expression of astonishment.

"You are sure? asked the judge.

"Yes."

"Do you ever sell strychnine indiscriminately over the counter?"

Alfred wilted visibly under the judge's frown.

"No—of course not. But, it was Mr. Inglethorp of Style's Lodge, and I thought it was okay. He said it was to poison some rats, that the lodge had an infestation."

The judge lowered her lids halfway, considering this.

"Did Mr. Inglethorp sign for the poison?"

"Yes."

"Have you got the book here?"

Albert Mace showed the book where Alfred signed for the strychnine, and then the judge dismissed him. Then, amidst a breathless silence, Alfred Inglethorp was called. Did he realize, I wondered, how closely the noose was drawn around his neck?

The judge went straight to the point.

"Last Monday evening, did you buy strychnine to poison some rats?"

Perfectly calm, Alfred responded, "No, I did not. Styles Resort doesn't have a rat problem."

"You absolutely deny purchasing strychnine last Monday night?"

"I do."

"Do you also deny *this*?" The judge handed him the register with his signature.

"Yes. That's not my handwriting, and I can prove it." Alfred took an old envelope out of his pocket, and wrote his name on it, handing it to the judge. The judge studied it and said, "Yes, it is certainly dissimilar. But then, how do you explain Mr. Mace's statement?"

Alfred stroked his mustache, almost like he was trying to be a comic book villain. "Mr. Mace must have been mistaken."

The judge hesitated and then asked, "Mr. Inglethorp, can you please tell us where you were on the evening of Monday, July 16th?"

Alfred looked down at his lap, as if he was being punished. "I really can't remember."

"That is unacceptable," said the judge sharply. "Think again."

Alfred stared at the ceiling like it could give him the answer. "Okay. I was out walking."

"Where were you walking?"

"I don't remember."

The judge's face went steely. "Were you with anyone?"

"No."

"Did you meet anyone on your walk?"

"No."

"That is unfortunate." The judge gave him some serious side eye. "I assume you can't say where you were when Mr. Mace said you entered the shop to purchase strychnine?"

"If you would like to take it that way, yes."

"Be careful, Mr. Inglethorp."

Perle fidgeted nervously. "Holy Buckets. Does this imbecile *want* to be arrested?"

When the judge moved to the next point, Perle sighed in relief.

"You had a disagreement with your wife on Tuesday afternoon?"

"Excuse me," interrupted Alfred, "but that is incorrect. I was out the entire afternoon."

"Is there anyone who can testify to that?"

"No, but you have my word," Alfred said, his tone challenging.

"Hmm." The judge seemed ready to lean over and slap Alfred, but of course, she didn't do that.

"There are two witnesses who swear they heard your disagreement with Mrs. Inglethorp."

"Those witnesses were mistaken."

I was staggered by Alfred's self-assurance. Glancing at Perle, I noticed she wore an exalted expression which I could not understand. Was she at last convinced of Alfred Inglethorp's guilt?

"Mr. Inglethorp," said the judge, "you heard your wife's dying words repeated here. Can you explain them in any way?"

"Yes, of course."

"You can?"

"It's simple. You read my wife's last words as an accusation"—Alfred continued—"I think she was calling out to me."

The judge took a moment, then said, "Mr. Inglethorp, you poured out the tea, and took it to your wife that evening?"

"I poured it out, but I didn't take it to her. I meant to, but then Dr. Blake stopped by, so I put the tea on the hall table. When I came through a few minutes later, it was gone."

This statement might, or might not, be true, but it didn't seem to improve much for Alfred. At any rate, he had plenty of time to poison her tea.

Perle nudged me gently, indicating a man who sat near the door. He was almost completely bald and had a large, wide nose. Not conventionally handsome, yet he had a strong presence that made him fun to look at.

I silently questioned Perle. She put her lips to my ear.

"Do you know who that man is?"

I shook my head.

"That is Detective James Jakes—Jimmy Jakes from the FBI. Things are moving quickly, my friend."

Now I openly stared. He felt my eyes on him, turned, and met my gaze. And—wait, had he just winked at me? If so, that was very un-FBI-like of him. I was still staring when I was startled by the judge giving the verdict:

"Cause of death: willful murder."

SEVEN

PERLE WORKS WITH THE FBI

As we left the inquest, Perle pulled me aside so we could wait for Inspector Jakes. He emerged after a few short moments, and Perle stepped forward, nearly accosting him. "Do you remember me, Inspector Jakes?"

His grin was as wide as his nose. "Perle Olsen. Of course I remember you. I learned more from you and your investigations class than I did in any of my other coursework." He grasped Perle's hand and gave it a firm shake. "How are you?"

"Good, good. I read about your employment with the FBI. Congratulations."

"Thank you." Inspector Jakes turned his gaze toward me. "I don't believe we've met. I'm Jimmy Jakes."

"Oh!" Perle exclaimed, in an overdone gesture of surprise. "How rude that I forgot to introduce you." She put her hand on my shoulder but spoke to him. "This is Helen, another former brilliant student of mine. Helen came through the program a few years after you."

"Ah," Jimmy Jakes said. "Nice to meet you. Are you police?"

"No," I replied. I felt my cheeks flush, and I had no idea why I was embarrassed. "I'm a security guard at the state capitol."

"*Mon ami* Helen is a hero! Perhaps you read about her in the papers? After the riots?"

Jakes furrowed his brow and opened his mouth, probably to ask Perle for more information about my supposed heroism. Hating the spotlight, I quickly interjected. "What did you think of the inquest? You must think it's serious if the FBI is here to investigate."

"Yeah, I'd say it's serious. You have the wealthy Cavendish family, and John's a state senator, and Emily Styles is pretty notorious around these parts. The whole thing could easily blow up and get out of control, with conspiracy theories and what not. We want a quick resolution. Luckily, it looks like we'll get one."

Perle said gravely, "I disagree. Helen was there when Emily died, and she and I conducted our own investigation immediately after. We can help you, you know."

A flicker of annoyance passed over Jakes's face, but it quickly morphed into resignation. "Alright. Since I trust your judgment, please enlighten me."

"Well, I will tell you this. If you arrest Mr. Inglethorp, it will bring you no kudos—the case against him will be dismissed at once! *Voila!*" And she snapped her fingers expressively.

Jakes gave an incredulous snort. As for me, I was literally dumb with astonishment. I worried Perle had gone mad.

Jakes tugged at his jacket collar, like he was heated. Except, it was a breezy day. "Can you give me a little more to go on?"

Perle sighed. "Come with us to Styles Resort. Alfred Inglethorp will probably refuse to talk to you. But I will give you proof, and you will see that the case against him can't be sustained. Is that a bargain?"

"That's a bargain," said Jakes heartily. "Except, I have to meet with the coroner first, so I will meet you there later. I confess that I can't see the faintest possible loophole in the evidence, but you always were a wonder! So long, then, Perle." He looked at me. "And it was nice to meet you, Helen."

I mumbled something like, "Same here," and he strode away.

"Well, my friend," cried Perle, before I could get in a word, "what do you think? I believe Alfred Inglethorp is an imbecile."

"There are other explanations besides imbecility," I remarked. "If the case against him is true, how could he defend himself except by silence?"

"Why, in a thousand ingenious ways," cried Perle. She looped her arm through mine, and we walked together. The sun was out, and spring was in the air. "If I'd committed this murder, I could think of at least seven stories that are more convincing than Alfred's stony denials!"

I could not help laughing.

"Only seven? I am sure you could think up seventy! But seriously, you can't still believe in Alfred's innocence?"

"Why not? Nothing has changed."

"But the evidence is so conclusive."

"Yes, too conclusive."

We turned in at the parking lot, where I'd left my car.

"Yes, yes, too conclusive," continued Perle, almost to herself. "Real evidence is usually vague and unsatisfactory. It has to be examined—sifted. But here the whole thing is cut and dried. No, my friend, this evidence has been very cleverly manufactured—so cleverly that it has defeated its own ends."

I unlocked the car, and we climbed in. Buckling her seatbelt, Perle said, "Look at it this way. A man sets out to poison his wife. He is not a total fool. He boldly purchases strychnine under his own name, with a trumped-up story about rats, which is ridiculous, especially when Emily, a resort owner, must have employed a pest control service. Anyway, Alfred does not use the poison that night. No, he waits until he has had a heated argument with her, when everyone can hear, and then they all suspect him. He prepares no defense—no shadow of an alibi, and he knows there's a record that he bought poison. Do not ask me to believe that any man could be so idiotic! Only a self-punishing lunatic would act that way!"

"Still—I do not see—" I began.

"--the answer?!" Perle interjected. "*Mon ami* Helen, it puzzles me too."

I'd been sitting behind the wheel, too stumped to start the car. But finally, I turned the key in the ignition and pulled away. The inquest had been performed in Grand Marais, and I drove through the lovely little town, past art galleries and along the lakeshore. "I mean, if he's innocent, how do you explain his buying the strychnine?"

"Simple. He did *not* buy it."

"But Mace recognized him!"

"I beg your pardon," Perle spoke without irony. "He saw a man with a long beard, a waxed mustache, wearing glasses and dressed in Alfred's rather noticeable clothes. But Mr. Mace was new to town."

"Then you think—"

"Suppose someone wished to pass himself off as John or Lawrence Cavendish. Would it be easy?"

"No," I said thoughtfully. "Of course, an actor—"

But Perle ruthlessly cut me short. "They are both clean-shaven men. Not so with Alfred Inglethorp. His clothes, his facial hair, the glasses which hide his eyes—those are the striking points about his appearance. Now, what is a criminal's first instinct? To divert suspicion from himself! He does that by throwing it onto someone else. Everybody already believed that Alfred was guilty. It was a foregone conclusion that he would be suspected, but, to make it a sure thing, there must be tangible proof—like the actual buying of the poison, and with a man who looks like Alfred, that was not difficult. Remember, that Mace guy never actually spoke to Alfred. So, why would he doubt that it was him, there to buy poison?"

"Okay," I said. "But, if that was the case, why didn't he say where he was at six o'clock on Monday evening?"

Perle gazed out the window. "If he were arrested, he probably would speak. If he did not murder his wife, he has something of his own to conceal, quite apart from the murder."

"Yeah, but what? If it was adultery, well sure, that would look bad, and prosecutors could argue motive. But it could also give him an alibi."

"Come, my friend," Perle said, changing the subject, "apart from Alfred, how did the evidence at the inquest strike you?"

"Oh, pretty much what I expected."

"You didn't notice anything unusual?"

"Like what?"

"Well, Lawrence's suggestion that his mother might have been poisoned accidentally from her sleep tonic, that did not strike you as strange?"

"Not really. I know the doctors thought it was ridiculous, but it was an easy mistake."

"Perhaps, for a normal person without a medical background. But you told me that Lawrence went to med school. Lawrence would probably understand the symptoms of strychnine poisoning, and yet he alone believes Emily died from natural causes."

"It's very confusing," I agreed.

"Then there is Mary," continued Perle. "She is not very forth-coming. What do you make of her attitude?"

"I don't know what to make of it. It's almost like she's trying to protect Alfred, but that makes no sense."

Perle nodded reflectively. "One thing is certain; she overheard a good deal more of that 'private conversation' than she was willing to admit." Perle rubbed the back of her neck absently. "And then there's Dr. Blake. What was *he* doing up and dressed at that hour in the morning? I'm shocked no one questioned it."

"Because he's creepy?"

Perle laughed. "His creepiness is a symptom, and not the cause."

I wasn't completely sure what she meant, so I replied, "He says he has insomnia."

"Which is a very good, or a very bad explanation," remarked Perle. "It covers everything and explains nothing."

"Anything else?"

"*Mon ami*," replied Perle gravely, "when you find that people are not telling you the truth—look out! I believe only one, possibly two, people told the truth at the inquest today."

"Oh, come now, Perle. What about John and Evie? I think they were both honest."

"Both of them? One, I grant you, but both?!"

Her words gave me an unpleasant shock. I trusted John, and if I couldn't, then I needed to reexamine a lot of my recent choices. And Evie was so straightforward that I never thought to doubt her sincerity.

"Do you really think so?" I asked. I wasn't ready for Perle's take on John, so I said, "Evie seems fundamentally honest—almost uncomfortably so."

Perle started to speak, and then checked herself.

"Cynthia too," I continued, "there's nothing dishonest about *her*."

"No. But it was strange that she never heard a sound, sleeping next door; but Mary, several rooms away, distinctly heard the table fall."

"Well, she's young. And she sleeps soundly."

"Ah, yes, indeed! She must be a famous sleeper, that one!"

I didn't like her sarcastic tone, but at that moment, I pulled into the drive at Styles Resort.

John came running out to greet us, holding his phone. "It's a feeding frenzy. Twitter, Facebook, and mainstream media, everyone is posting about us."

Pictures of the family leaving the inquest accompanied headlines like, "It's Murder! Wealthy, Political Family Kills Their Own." Or, "Who Killed Emily Styles? Five Reasons Her Family Wanted Her Dead."

"Oh John, I'm so sorry," I said.

"Do not worry," Perle told him. "Soon, Inspector Jakes will arrive, and we can get to the bottom of this. The innocent have nothing to fear."

John's already gray face turned a new shade of ashen. He couldn't respond, but just pressed his lips together.

Perle, seemingly oblivious, said, "I must prepare the room. We will all meet when Jakes gets here."

She walked past, without waiting for approval from John. I wanted to offer something, anything, to make it better, but couldn't come up with much. "Don't look at your phone," I said. "It will just make you crazy."

"Everything is making me crazy," he replied, looking past me, to where Perle strode off a moment ago.

"Right. I should, umm, go help."

Around twenty minutes later, Jakes showed up. When he walked into the room set up by Perle, I was alone. Perle was in the kitchen, fetching a pitcher of water and cups, because "Occasions like this can be tense, and people might get thirsty."

"Hello," Jakes said, with warmth in his voice.

"Hi!" Involuntarily, my hand went to my hair, smoothing and tucking a lock behind my ear. "You're here so soon."

"The coroner didn't take long." He looked around at all the chairs. "What do you have planned?"

"It's all Perle's idea. She has something to pronounce, I believe."

Jakes laughed softly to himself. "Okay. I guess she's doing my job for me, then?"

"I know she's eccentric, but she's seldom wrong."

Jakes looked me squarely in the eye. "Perle Olsen is brilliant. I recognize that. As long as she doesn't subvert FBI protocol, I'll give her free reign."

At that moment, Perle walked in. "Ah, Inspector Jakes. You are here. Your promptness speaks well for you."

Perle called everyone together, and stood before us all, bowing as though she were a magician about to perform an illusion. Everyone sat, except for Jakes, who leaned against a wall in the back, and me, who stood off to the side. Perle, of course, took center stage. "I have asked you to come here all together, for a specific reason, which concerns Alfred Inglethorp."

Alfred sat by himself—I think, unconsciously, everyone had pulled their chairs slightly away from him—and he gave a faint start as Perle said his name.

"Alfred," said Perle, addressing him directly, "a very dark shadow is resting on this house—the shadow of murder."

Alfred shook his head sadly.

"My poor wife," he murmured. "Poor Emily! It is terrible."

Perle crossed her arms over her chest and shook her head. "You do not realize the gravity of your situation." Alfred did not appear to comprehend. Perle lowered her voice, adding in a near hiss, "You are in very grave danger."

Jakes fidgeted. I saw Miranda rights hovering on his lips, but he kept silent.

Perle continued. "Do you understand now?" She waited expectantly, but Alfred was sloth-like with his response.

"No." He wrinkled his forehead. "What do you mean?"

Seriously? How dense could the man be?

Perle's nostrils flared in exasperation. She dropped the theatrics and spoke plainly. "I mean that you are suspected of poisoning your wife."

A little gasp ran through the room.

Alfred shot up. "Oh, I see. It's always the husband, is that right? Well, I loved Emily and I did not poison her."

"Sit down!" For such a tiny woman, Perle adopted a tremendously imposing demeanor. Alfred did as she said.

She pointed at his chest. "Do you realize how guilty you seemed at the inquest? Let me put it this way; be glad that Minnesota doesn't have the death penalty. Even still, I suggest you say where you were at six o'clock on Monday evening."

With a groan, Alfred sank down again and buried his face in his hands. Perle approached and stood over him.

"Speak!" she cried menacingly.

With an effort, Alfred raised his face from his hands. Then, slowly and deliberately, he shook his head.

"You will not speak?"

"No. Only a monster would accuse me of what you say."

Perle nodded thoughtfully; she was a woman with her mind made up. "Then I will speak for you."

Alfred Inglethorp sprang up again.

"You? How can you speak? You do not know——" he broke off abruptly.

Perle turned to face the rest of the room. "Listen up! The man who purchased strychnine at six o'clock last Monday was not Alfred Inglethorp." Perle paused, enjoying the moment's drama. A smile played at her lips, but she suppressed it, like an actress who found her own lines amusing. "You see, at six o'clock on that day, Alfred was with Janet Raikes. I can produce no fewer than five witnesses who swear they saw them together. There is absolutely no question as to the alibi!"

EIGHT

FRESH SUSPICIONS

There was a moment of stupefied silence. Jakes was the first to speak.

"Incredible," he cried, "you're the real deal! But Perle, these witnesses of yours are legit, right?"

"*Voilà!* I have prepared a list of them—names and addresses. You must speak with them, of course."

"Certainly." Jakes lowered his voice. "I really appreciate it. Arresting him would have been a hot mess." He turned to Alfred. "But why didn't you say this at the inquest?"

"I know why," interrupted Perle. "There's a rumor going around—"

"A maliciously false rumor!" Alfred cried.

"And Alfred was anxious to avoid scandal. Am I right?"

"Exactly." Alfred nodded. "I didn't want them spreading any more lies."

Jakes met my eye, we shared a moment of understanding, and I knew we were of the same mind. "Between you and me," he remarked to Alfred, "I'd rather people lie about me than be arrested for murder. And I assume your poor wife would have felt the same.

And if it hadn't been for Perle, I would have arrested you before you could say 'not guilty!'"

"I get it," murmured Alfred. "But you don't understand how I have been persecuted and maligned." He shot Evie a searing look.

Jakes turned briskly to John, "I'd like to see Emily's bedroom, please, and afterward, I'll talk with Dorcas."

John swallowed roughly. I noticed a tiny bead of sweat on his forehead. "I'll take you."

"Don't worry about it. Perle here will show me the way."

As they filed out, Perle turned and made a sign for me to follow her upstairs. Then she caught me by the arm and drew me aside.

"Quick, go to the other end of the hall. Just stand there—do not move till I come." Then, turning rapidly, she rejoined Jakes.

I followed her instructions, feeling about as awkward as a kid at a middle school dance. Why on earth did I need to stand here? Then it occurred to me: with the exception of Cynthia, everyone's room was over here. Even though I didn't understand, I stood faithfully at my post. It wasn't terribly unlike being a security guard most of the time. The minutes passed. Nobody came. Nothing happened.

It was nearly twenty minutes before Perle approached.

"You've been here the whole time?"

"I've stuck here like a rock. Nothing's happened."

"Ah!" Was she pleased, or disappointed? "You've seen nothing at all?"

"No."

"But you have probably heard something? A big bump—eh, *mon ami?*"

"No."

"But I knocked over the nightstand. Not on purpose, of course. It's quite embarrassing."

I instantly wanted to console her. "It's not your fault. Everyone is overexcited from what you said downstairs. What are you going to do now? Where is Jakes?"

"He's interviewing Dorcas. I showed him all our exhibits. I am disappointed in Jakes. He has no method!"

"Oh," I said. Even though I barely knew him, I was instantly offended on Jake's behalf. Looking for a distraction, I peered out the window. "Dr. Blake is down there, creepy as ever."

"He is unusual," observed Perle meditatively.

"Unusual and annoying. It was funny to see him covered in mud on Tuesday." I described how he'd fallen while looking for a fern. "He looked ridiculous."

"You saw him, then?"

"Yes. Of course, he didn't want to come in—it was just after dinner—but Alfred insisted."

"What?" Perle caught me violently by the shoulders. "Was Dr. Blake here on Tuesday evening? Here? And you never told me? Why did you not tell me? Why? Why?"

A flush crept up Perle's neck, and she broke out in a sweat.

"Perle, are you okay?" I nearly started to remind her that Albert had mentioned Dr. Blake's presence here on Tuesday night during his testimony, and that Perle must have been distracted by noticing Jimmy Jakes and she didn't hear.

But she looked unwell, and the last thing Perle needed was to be told that she'd missed a detail.

She took several deep breaths and rapidly tugged at her collar, like she was fanning herself. "Hot flash," she explained. "They are triggered by acute stress."

"Perle, I'm sorry. I didn't realize it was so important."

"Of course it's important! So, Dr. Blake was here on Tuesday night—the night of the murder. Helen, do you not see? That changes everything—everything!"

I'd never seen her so worked up. She loosened her hold on me, stepped away, and found a pair of candlesticks to mechanically straighten, still murmuring to herself, "Yes, that changes everything—everything." Suddenly she came to a decision. "We must go. Now. You're driving." She grabbed her bag, checked the inside of it, and apparently satisfied, shut the flap.

"Where are we going?" I asked, once we were in the car.

"Back to Grand Marias." She took out her phone and recited the address. Then she made a call, something about ordering a test. When she was done, I said,

"Perle, will you tell me what this is all about?"

She took a spritzer bottle from her purse and sprayed her hair and face. Then she took a tissue and wiped away the mixture of mist and lingering sweat. "In ten years or so, Helen, you will want to always carry both a spray bottle and a handkerchief with you. They are invaluable tools, post-hot flash."

"Noted," I replied. I almost told her that for me, menopause should be at least fifteen years away, but I didn't want to sound petty. "Anyway, what's going on?"

"Well, since Alfred is no longer a suspect, we must figure out who bought the poison. Who impersonated him? We also have his statement that he put the tea down in the hall. No one took much notice of that at the inquest—but now it has a very different significance. We must find out who took Emily her tea. From what you said, the only ones who definitely did *not* take it were Mary and Cynthia."

"Yes, that's right."

She turned to me abruptly. "Tell me, Helen, is there anyone you suspect?"

I hesitated. To tell the truth, I had a wild idea that I dismissed as ridiculous. But the idea was stubborn and kept returning. "I don't know if it's worth mentioning," I said.

"Ah, Helen. Speak your mind. You should always pay attention to your instincts."

"Okay," I blurted out, "it's crazy, but I don't think Evie is saying everything that she knows!"

I waited for Perle to start laughing at me. Instead, she simply said, "Explain."

"We didn't include her in the list of possible suspects simply because she wasn't there that night. But she was only a thirty-minute drive away. Can we say for sure that she wasn't at Styles on the night of the murder?"

"Yes, we can. Evie posted a photo on Facebook, of her with friends at the lighthouse bridge in Duluth. It checks out."

"Oh!" I said, a bit deflated. "Well," I continued, "even still, she hates Alfred so much, and that's what I find suspicious. I can't help feeling she'd do anything to hurt him."

"Are you suggesting Evie framed Alfred for murder?"

I gripped the steering wheel. That hadn't occurred to me. "Not necessarily. But she might know something about Emily's will. She … I don't know. I mean, they're related, and if there's such bad blood between them, I don't get why he showed up at Styles in the first place. She's so bitter toward him."

"Bitter to the point of insanity?" Perle cocked her head, inquisitive.

"Perhaps."

At that, I could instantly sense Perle's response. She shook her head energetically. "No, no, you are on the wrong track. Evie seems quintessentially sane. She has a mind like a steel trap."

Hadn't Perle just told me to trust my instincts? I sucked in a breath. "Sure, but she's almost manic in her hatred toward Alfred. I know it's a crazy idea, but what if she meant to poison Alfred, and somehow Emily got hold of it by mistake?"

"I don't think that is possible." Perle placed a gentle hand on my shoulder. *"Mon ami* Helen, you are correct to suspect everyone. Do not mistake my disagreement with disregard. So, let's go through this idea, point by point. How do we know Evie did not poison Emily on purpose?

"Because she was devoted to her!" I exclaimed.

In an instant, Perle went from being a patient teacher to a scolding one. If she had a ruler, she would have slapped me on the wrist. "That's a naive argument. If Evie could poison Emily, she would be quite equally capable of simulating devotion."

"Sorry," I muttered.

"Do not apologize," Perle quipped. "Anyway, we must look elsewhere. You are correct to assume that her vehemence against Alfred Inglethorp is too violent to be natural, but you are quite wrong in the deduction you draw from it. I have drawn my own deductions, which I believe to be correct, but I won't say them, not just yet." She paused a minute, then went on. "Now, to my way of thinking, there is one reason that Evie could not have murdered Emily, and there's no getting around it."

"And that is?"

"That in no possible way did Emily's death benefit Evie. There is no murder without a motive."

I reflected. "What if Evie is named in Emily's will?"

Perle shook her head. "No. I have my own opinion about the will. But I can tell you this much—it was not in Evie's favor."

I accepted this, though I didn't see how she could be so sure. "Well," I said, with a sigh, "we will acquit Evie, then. It is partly your fault that I began to suspect her. It was what you said about her evidence at the inquest that set me off."

Perle looked puzzled.

"What did I say about her evidence at the inquest?"

"Don't you remember? When I cited her and John Cavendish as being above suspicion?"

"Oh—ah—yes." She seemed a little confused but recovered quickly. "By the way, Helen, there is something I want you to do for me."

"Sure. What is it?"

"Next time you are alone with Lawrence Cavendish, I want you to say, 'I have a message for you, from Perle. She says to find the extra teacup, and you can rest in peace!' Nothing more. Nothing less."

"'Find the extra teacup, and you can rest in peace.' Is that right?" I asked, mystified.

"Excellent."

"But what does it mean?"

"Ah, that I will leave you to find out. You have access to the facts. Just say that to him and see what he says."

"Sure—but it's all so mysterious."

We were on the edge of Grand Marias now, and Perle directed me to the U.S Drug Testing Center.

I pulled into the parking lot. "I'll be right back," Perle said briskly, and went inside. In a few minutes, she was back again.

"There," she said. "All done."

"What were you doing there?" I asked, nearly bursting with curiosity.

"I left something to be analyzed."

"Yes, but what?"

"The sample of cocoa I took from Emily's cup."

"Dr. Blake had it tested already, and you laughed at the possibility of there being strychnine in it."

"I know Dr. Blake had it tested," replied Perle quietly.

"Well, then?"

"Well, I wanted it analyzed again, and that is all."

She clamped her mouth shut, and I realized that I was getting nothing more from her on the subject.

Emily's funeral took place the following day, and on Monday, as I came downstairs for breakfast, John pulled me aside. "Alfred is gone. It's such a relief. Everything's been so awkward between us. It was bad enough when we thought he was guilty. Now that we know he's not, I kept wondering if I should apologize, but I couldn't bring myself to say anything. Anyway, he's welcome to Emily's money, but thank God he doesn't get Styles Resort."

"You'll be able to keep up the place all right?" I asked.

"I suppose. Half of my father's money goes with the place, and Lawrence will stay here for now, so there is his share as well. We'll have to tighten our belts, but I think everything will work out."

Alfred's absence definitely lightened the mood. At breakfast, Cynthia told jokes. Lawrence was his usual gloomy self, but the rest of us could even laugh about the media's relentless obsession with 'The Murder at Styles Resort,' and their rubbernecking at the tragedy. #Murder@Styles was constantly trending.

Dorcas came up to me after breakfast.

"Something occurred to me. You remember how Perle asked about a green garment?"

"Sure."

"There's a box upstairs, with old Halloween costumes. There might be a green dress in it."

"Oh. Thank you, Dorcas."

I was in such a good mood, feeling more relaxed than I had in a while, so much so that I almost didn't text Perle and tell her to come over and investigate that box. Then, I remembered how Perle reacted when I forgot to tell her about Dr. Blake, and her insistence that every detail matters.

Reluctantly, I texted, and she came straight over.

"Is Jakes here?" she asked, by way of saying hello.

Fact was, Jakes came and went quite a bit, investigating and questioning. None of us knew exactly what he was after, not even me. The other day, he suggested we sit for a cup of coffee while we compared notes of our law enforcement careers. He wanted me to tell him my story of the capital riots. "It wasn't as big a thing as the press makes it out to be," I said.

"You're too modest," he insisted, and that wide smile invaded his face. Were we becoming friends?

"He's not here yet," I told Perle now. "Follow me. Dorcas already showed me where the box is."

I led her to the attic storage area. "There it is," I said, pointing at it.

Perle bundled everything out on the floor with little ceremony. There were one or two green fabrics of varying shades, but Perle shook her head over them all. She seemed a bit apathetic, as if she didn't expect to find anything fruitful. Then suddenly, she gave an exclamation.

"What is it?"

"Look!"

The chest was nearly empty, and there, right at the bottom, was a magnificent false mustache and beard, just like Alfred's, only made from synthetic hair.

"My goodness," said Perle, inspecting it. "It seems quite new."

"Do you think it is *the* beard and mustache?" I whispered eagerly.

Perle nodded. "I do. You see how it's been shaped?"

"No."

She showed it to me. "There's even a bit of fresh wax, and a couple of snipped hairs. Helen, this is a notable discovery."

"I wonder who put it in the chest."

"Someone intelligent," Perle remarked. "Whoever it was, they chose the one place in the house to hide it where its presence would not be noticed. Yes, the person is intelligent. But we must be more intelligent. We must be so intelligent that we are not suspected of being intelligent at all."

"Okay," I agreed, nodding my head. But my brain swam, and I felt the opposite of intelligent.

"Helen, you will be a huge help to me."

I beamed at the compliment. Just when I thought Perle didn't appreciate me at all.

But then, she burst my bubble. "However, I need an ally in the house."

"You have me," I protested.

"True, but you are not sufficient."

I was hurt and showed it. Perle reached out, like she was erasing something.

"You misunderstand. Everyone knows we're working together. I need an ally who isn't associated with us at all."

"Oh, I see. How about John?"

"Not John," she stated flatly.

"Hmm." I voiced what I'd thought for a while. "He's got good social skills, but perhaps he isn't super bright." I said it thoughtfully, as if I could cushion the words. "I think he's succeeded in a way that's exclusive to rich, white men."

"Evie," Perle said, clearly not having heard a word I said. "My ally must be Evie. Let's go find her."

Evie was in Emily's office, sitting at her old desk, apparently going through a record book of some kind. Perle closed the door behind us.

Evie scowled. "I'm busy. What do you need?"

Perle answered. "Do you remember that I once asked you to help me?"

"Yes, I do." Evie nodded. "And I said I would help bring Alfred Inglethorp to justice."

"I see. So let me ask you a simple question: Do you still believe that Alfred poisoned Emily?"

"Good heavens!" cried Evie. "Do you really need to ask? That man is the devil incarnate. I said he'd murder her in her bed, and I was right. I hate him like the poison he used to murder Emily."

"Excellent," Perle said, as if Evie had just scored well on an exam. "And do you remember saying that if anyone you loved was murdered, you'd know instinctually who did it, even if you were unable to prove it?"

"Yes, I remember saying that. I believe it too. I suppose you think I'm crazy?"

"Not at all."

"And yet you ignored my instinct against Alfred Inglethorp."

"No," said Perle curtly. "Because your instinct is not against Alfred Inglethorp."

"What?" Evie's red face pivoted back and forth, like she was hearing voices.

Perle slowly walked to the seat opposite Emily's desk, and gently lowered herself into the chair. "You want to believe he committed the crime. You believe he's capable of it. But your instinct tells you he did *not* commit it. It tells you more—shall I go on?"

Evie stared at Perle, fascinated, and she made a slight affirmative movement with her hand.

"We all try to believe what we want to believe. But you are trying to drown and stifle your instinct, which tells you someone else—"

"No, no, no!" cried Evie wildly, flinging up her hands. "Don't say it! It isn't true! It can't be true. I don't know what put such a wild—such a horrific—idea into my head!"

"So, am I correct?" Perle asked

"Yes, yes; you must be psychic to have guessed. But it's too monstrous, too impossible. It *must* be Alfred Inglethorp."

Perle shook her head. "I—I, too, have an instinct. We are working together toward a common end."

"Don't ask me to help you, because I won't. I wouldn't lift a finger to—to—" She faltered.

Perle stared into Evie's eyes like she could melt her brain. "You will help me despite yourself. You will be my ally. You will not be able to help yourself. You will do the only thing that I want of you."

Evie bowed her head. "It could be hushed up."

"There must be no hushing up."

"But Emily herself—" She broke off.

"Evie," said Perle gravely, "this is unworthy of you."

"Yes," she said quietly, and gave a resigned sigh. "It's time to be on the side of justice!"

And with these words, she walked firmly out of the room.

"There," said Perle, looking after her, "goes a very valuable ally. That woman, Helen, has brains as well as a heart."

I did not reply.

"Instinct is a marvelous thing," mused Perle. "It can neither be explained nor ignored."

"You and Evie both know what you are talking about," I observed coldly. "Yet *I* am still in the dark."

"Really? Is that so, *mon ami?*"

"Yes. Enlighten me, will you?"

Perle studied me attentively for a moment or two. Then, to my intense surprise, she shook her head.

"No, my friend."

My mouth dropped open. It took me a second to form words. "Seriously? Why not?"

"Two is enough for a secret."

Pure, hot anger surged through me. "That's unfair. I can't believe that after everything, you would withhold facts."

"I am not withholding facts. Every fact I know is in your possession. You can draw your own deductions from them. This time it is a question of ideas."

"Then tell me your ideas."

Perle looked at me very earnestly, and again shook her head.

"You see," she said sadly, "*you* have no instincts."

That stung. Perle had once called me her "most brilliant student." But I wouldn't concede to the pain. I held my ground. "You were looking for intelligence just now," I pointed out.

"The two often go together," said Perle.

Ouch. Was she saying that I lacked both instinct *and* intelligence? Perhaps Perle was one more person who, when she looked at me, ultimately saw disappointment. Just like Paul. Just like myself, when I looked in the mirror.

Suddenly, I needed some space away from Perle. "I see," I replied. "Well, good luck, Perle." Before she could respond, I walked away.

I resolved to make my own interesting and important discoveries, and when I did, I would keep them to myself. Perle would ultimately be surprised by my instinct and intelligence.

It was time to assert myself.

NINE

DR. BLAKE

It was another gorgeous day, unseasonably warm. Spring had decided to come early to the north shore. I strolled along the lawn, which was still soggy. Yet that hadn't stopped Lawrence from taking out the croquet balls and mallet. He aimlessly whacked wooden balls around.

I realized that I'd never delivered Perle's message, and decided that now would be a good time. Perhaps I could decode Lawrence's response and use some cross-examination and deduction to make a significant observation. I went right up to him.

"I've been looking for you," I said, maybe a bit too loud.

"You have?" Lawrence stopped swinging his mallet and gave me a skeptical look. "Why?"

"I've got a message for you from Perle."

"Okay. And?"

"She said to wait until we were alone." I dropped my voice significantly, and watched him intently out of the corner of my eye. I liked to think I was good at creating an atmosphere.

"Well?" His gloomy expression didn't change.

"This is the message." I whispered. "'Find the extra teacup, and you can rest in peace.'"

"What on earth does she mean?" Lawrence widened his eyes, clearly confused.

"You don't know?"

"Nope. Do you?"

I shook my head.

"What extra teacup?"

"I don't know." I straightened my shoulders, trying to mask my embarrassment. "Okay, I'll tell Perle that you didn't understand." I walked off toward the lodge when he suddenly called me back.

"Helen, say the message over again, will you?"

"'Find the extra teacup, and you can rest in peace.' Are you sure you don't know what it means?"

"No, I don't. I—I wish I did." He sighed and dropped his mallet. "Maybe I'm just hungry. Should we go eat lunch?"

"Sure."

We walked to the house together. In the dining room, I discovered that John had invited Perle to stay for a sandwich. She already sat at the table. I gave her a frosty hello.

Perle barely noticed. Once everyone sat around the table, eating contentedly, she suddenly leaned in toward Mary.

"Mary, I'm sorry to bring up unpleasant memories, but I have a little idea and would like to ask one or two questions."

"Of me? Certainly."

"Thank you. I just want to know if the door leading into Emily's room from Cynthia's was bolted?"

"On the night Emily died? Yes, it was bolted," replied Mary, surprised. "I said so at the inquest."

"Bolted?"

"Yes." She looked confused.

"I mean," explained Perle, "you are sure it was bolted, and not merely locked?"

"Oh, I see what you mean. No, I don't know. I said bolted, meaning that it was fastened, and I could not open it, but I believe all the doors were found bolted on the inside."

"So, the door might have simply been locked?"

"I suppose. I—never looked."

"But *I* did," interrupted Lawrence suddenly. "I happened to notice that it *was* bolted."

"Ah, that settles it." And Perle looked crestfallen.

For once, one of her ideas hadn't panned out, and I'll admit that I took some joy in it.

After lunch, Perle sweetly asked if I'd walk her back to her condo. I consented rather stiffly.

"Helen, are you upset with me?" she asked anxiously, as we walked along the beach.

"Not at all," I said coldly.

"Oh, good. I'm so relieved."

For someone who prided herself on her "instincts," Perle was bad at inferring my true feelings. Still, her earnest concern thawed me a bit.

"I gave Lawrence your message," I said.

"And what did he say? He was completely confused?"

"Yes. He had no idea what you meant."

I thought Perle would be disappointed; but, to my surprise, she said, "Good, good. That is what I thought."

My pride forbade me to ask any questions.

Perle changed the subject. "Where was Cynthia today?"

"She went back to work at the pharmacy."

"That's right. I forgot about her job." Perle rubbed at the back of her neck. "How often does she work?

"Every day except Wednesday and Saturday afternoon."

"I would love to see the pharmacy. Do you think she'd show it to me?"

"I expect that she will. She's quite proud of the work she does."

"As she should be. After all, it is very responsible work. I suppose they have very strong drugs there? Things like henbane and warafin, which can be lethal if used incorrectly. Or, I suppose, there's this maqianzi that Lawrence mentioned?"

I didn't want to admit my ignorance about the specific poisons that are still used for medicinal purposes. "Yes, she showed them to us. The really powerful ones are kept locked up in a little cabinet. They have to be very careful. They always take out the key before leaving the room."

"Of course. It is near the window, this cabinet?"

"No, right on the other side of the room. Why?"

Perle shrugged. "Just curious. Will you come in?"

We had reached her condo.

"No. I feel like taking a walk through the woods."

Perle widened her eyes at my rejection, but then she nodded and said, "Enjoy your walk."

I was determined to.

The woods around Styles Resort were very beautiful. After the walk across the beach, it was pleasant to saunter lazily through the cool glades. There was hardly a breath of wind, and the very chirp of the birds was faint and subdued. I strolled a little and finally sat on the stump of an old tree. The sun's rays hit me just right, and in my jacket, I was plenty warm. There was a large tree trunk that I could relax my head against. Suddenly, I was at peace with the world. Then I yawned.

I could forgive Perle for her secrecy, and even for her insults. Emily's murder seemed unreal and far away. Only the beauty of my surroundings mattered.

I yawned again.

My mind drifted and I guess I dozed off, because I dreamt that Emily was alive, and Lawrence had murdered Alfred Inglethorp with a croquet mallet. Then, John got so worked up that he shouted, "No! We can't go on like this!"

I woke up with a start.

Oh no.

With horror, I realized almost instantly that about twelve feet away from me, John and Mary Cavendish stood, facing each other. They were in the middle of a marital spat, and this was super awkward. The tree I leaned against hid my presence, and before I could move or speak, John repeated the words which woke me from my dream.

"I'm telling you Mary, we can't go on like this."

Mary's voice came, cool and liquid. "*We* can't go on like this? Come on John, say what you mean."

"Fine. My mother's funeral was on Saturday, and here you are, running around with Dr. Blake. It's embarrassing."

"So, you're worried about your image."

"Not just that. He bugs me. There's something very strange about him."

"He's a brilliant doctor, John. You wouldn't understand, since you're simply a trust-fund, third-rate politician."

Fire in her eyes, ice in her voice. The blood rose to John's face in a crimson tide.

"Mary!"

"Well?" Her tone did not change.

His response sounded so defeated. "You're still going to see him, no matter what I say?"

"If I feel like it, yes." She stepped in, like she was about to charge him. "It's not like you're in any position to pass judgment."

John stumbled back, growing pale. "What do you mean?" he said, his voice trembling.

"You know exactly what I mean!" Mary nearly whispered. "You *do* see, don't you, that *you* have no right to say anything to me?"

John's eyes pleaded with her. "No right? Have I *no* right, Mary?" His voice contained tears. He stretched out his hands. "Mary———"

For a moment, I thought she wavered. A softer expression came over her face, then suddenly she turned almost fiercely away.

"None!"

She began to walk away, but John sprang after her and caught her by the arm.

"Mary"—his voice was very quiet now—"are you in love with Blake?"

She hesitated. Across her face swept an expression full of mystery, sadness, and resignation.

She freed herself quietly from his arm and spoke over her shoulder. "I don't know," she said and then rushed off, leaving John standing there as though he had been turned to stone.

Now was the moment to save myself. I deliberately crackled some dead branches as I stood and made stomping noises. John turned. Luckily, he seemed to assume that I'd just arrived.

"Oh, hello, Helen!" He smiled, instantly composed. John was the consummate politician; no one would ever guess he was falling apart inside. "Did you walk Perle back to her condo? She's so interesting. But is she honestly a decent detective?"

"Her reputation is beyond reproach."

"I see. I hope you're right because I can't take much more of this."

"More of what?" I asked.

John sighed. "Well, to start, the only mother I ever knew died in front of me, and I couldn't help her. Now that FBI detective is in and out of the house; I never know when he'll turn up next. Meanwhile, Twitter and Facebook can't get enough of the whole mess, and every day there's a new conspiracy theory. And since I'm in politics, the journalists are relentless. And crowds gather every day, wanting to know why we aren't open for guests, when they all just want to come and play amateur sleuth."

"Cheer up, John!" I said soothingly. "It can't last forever."

"Logically, I know you're right, but emotionally, it seems unending. And that's not even the worst part." John lowered his voice. "Helen, I know you're helping Perle investigate, so you must wonder who did it. I know it couldn't have been an accident, but then that means that it had to be one of us."

For all his flaws, John was a decent man, and he'd only ever been kind to me. I had to say something to comfort him. Instantly, an idea clicked into place. With all of Perle's hints and innuendos, I couldn't believe I hadn't thought of it already. No wonder she thought I had no instinct, and so little intelligence.

"No, John," I said, "it isn't one of us. How could it be?"

"I know, but, still, who else is there?"

"Can't you guess?"

"No."

I looked cautiously round and lowered my voice.

"Dr. Blake!" I whispered.

His mouth fell open. "But why would he murder Emily? He had no motive."

"That's true," I confessed, "but I'll tell you this: Perle thinks so."

"Really? Did she tell you that?"

"Not exactly." Then, I told him about how worked up Perle became when I mentioned that Dr. Blake had been at Styles on the fatal night, and added, "She said twice: 'That changes everything.' And I've been thinking. You know Alfred said he put down the tea in the hall? That was right when Blake arrived. Isn't it possible that, as Alfred brought him through the hall, the doctor dropped something into the tea in passing?"

"Hmm," said John. "It would have been very risky."

"Yes, but it was possible."

"And then, how could he know it was her tea? Sorry, Helen. That just doesn't make sense."

Then I remembered something else.

"You're right. That wasn't how it was done. Listen." And I then told him about the cocoa sample which Perle took to be analyzed.

John questioned it, just like I had.

"I thought Blake already had the cocoa analyzed."

"Yeah, but you're missing the point! If Blake's the murderer, nothing could be easier than for him to substitute some ordinary cocoa for his sample and send that to be tested. And of course, they would find no strychnine! But no one would dream of suspecting Blake, or think of taking another sample—except Perle," I added, with belated recognition.

"Yes, but what about the bitter taste that cocoa won't disguise?"

"Well, we only have his word for that. And there are other possibilities. If he's one of the world's greatest toxicologists, perhaps he's found some way of making strychnine tasteless. Or it may not have been strychnine at all, but some obscure drug no one has ever heard of, which produces much the same symptoms."

"It's possible," said John. "But could he poison the cocoa? Wasn't it upstairs?"

"True," I admitted reluctantly.

A new idea invaded my brain. What if Dr. Blake had an accomplice? I prayed John wouldn't read my mind or sense the concern hanging off me. I glanced sideways at him, as we walked through the woods, twigs breaking beneath our feet. When we reached the clearing, Lake Superior back in view, the sun illuminated his face. His expression seemed guileless, and I breathed a sigh of relief.

But I didn't breathe easy for long. Memories ran through my mind: Mary, with a gleam in her eye, saying poison is a woman's weapon; Mary, arguing with Emily on Tuesday afternoon; Mary acting so restless on that fatal Tuesday evening. Had Emily discovered an affair between Mary and Dr. Blake, and had she threatened to tell John? Was that the motive?

Then I remembered that confusing argument between Evie and Perle. What if Mary's guilt was the monstrous possibility that Evie didn't want to believe?

Everything fit.

"There's another thing," said John suddenly, and the unexpected sound of his voice made me jump a little. "Something that doesn't make sense."

"What's that?" I asked.

"Dr. Blake told the paramedics they should perform an autopsy. Why would he do that, when he could have tried to pass Emily's death off as natural causes?"

"Perhaps he was playing the long game, and didn't want people wondering why a man of his reputation would call it heart disease."

"Yes, that's possible," admitted John. "Still," he added, "I don't see a motive."

I trembled.

"Look," I said, "I could be wrong. And remember, all this is in confidence."

"Oh, of course—that goes without saying."

As we approached the entrance to the lodge, Cynthia pulled up. When she got out, I said, "How was work?"

"It felt great to be back."

Wordlessly, John walked inside, but Cynthia and I stayed outside, soaking up the sun's rays.

"Perle was asking about the pharmacy. She wants a tour."

"Oh, sure. I'd love to show it to her. But she is a strange one, isn't she?"

"What do you mean?

Cynthia tossed her auburn hair off her shoulder. "The other day my collar was crooked, and she insisted on straightening it for me."

I laughed. "That sounds like Perle."

"Well, anyway, I should show her around soon, before I leave."

"You're leaving?"

Cynthia nodded. "The pharmacy up here doesn't pay as well as ones down in Duluth or Minneapolis would. And I'll need to pay for rent soon. Emily didn't provide for me, and I'm pretty sure Mary wants me out. I think she hates me."

"Really? But why?"

Cynthia shrugged. "I don't know. But she's not the only one. Lawrence hates me too."

"I doubt that."

"I don't." She sniffed back tears. "Have you ever felt alone, Helen?"

"All the time." I thought about sharing my own sad story, but I didn't have the energy, not at that moment. Then, a thought occurred to me. "Hey, if you want to move down to the cities, you could always stay with me for a while, until you figure everything out."

She smiled sadly. "You're sweet. But I couldn't impose on you like that."

Cynthia walked inside, and I followed, unsure of how to convince her that I'd welcome her company. In the lobby, John yelled at Evie. Lawrence stood nearby.

"What the hell? I can't think what the FBI is after! They've been in every room in the house—turning things inside out, and upside down. When I see Jakes again, I'll lay into him!"

Evie mumbled something unintelligible. Mary was silent, and Lawrence said, "Calm down. They're just making a show of doing something."

"Is Jakes around right now?" I asked.

"Lucky for him, he isn't," remarked John.

But I knew which coffee shop in Lutsen was Jakes' favorite. I could find him and see if he had any suspicions about Blake. "I think I'll drive into town," I said. I ran up to my room, grabbed my keys, and made a quick exit.

When I got to Common Grounds, the coffee shop where Jakes liked to hang out, I walked in, scanning the place for his shiny bald head and easy smile. But there were no customers.

The woman behind the counter, Amanda, knew me by now. "Hi, Helen, have you heard the big news?"

"No, what?"

"They took Dr. Blake!"

"What? Who's 'they'?"

"The police!" She pointed out the window. "He was walking down the street, when a cop car pulled up, arrested him, and drove off!" She beamed with pride at having told me the news. "We don't know what the charges are. But anyway, what can I get you?"

Out of politeness, I ordered a bottle of water. Then I tore out of there. I had to find Perle.

TEN

THE ARREST

To my extreme annoyance, Perle was not in. I knocked on her door and was met with silence, so then I texted her. *Where are you?*

Drove home to see family. Won't be answering any more texts tonight.

Perle had two college-aged daughters, and a husband who traveled a lot for work. She must have been having a family reunion of sorts, but geez, her timing was awful. Still, I knew there was no point in texting her back. She was hard enough to communicate with in person.

And where was Jakes? I supposed he was interrogating Blake.

Slowly, I walked back to the lodge. It was probably best to stay quiet, but I had to talk to someone. So, I found John. He let out a long whistle when I imparted the news.

"Wow, Helen. You *were* right, then. I couldn't believe it at the time."

"I understand. But once you think about it, everything makes sense. But, what do you think we should do now? I suppose the news won't be released until tomorrow."

John rubbed his chin. "Then let's wait. There's no need to say anything yet."

But to my intense surprise, there was not a word about the arrest on any of my favorite news sites! CNN had a column about "The Styles Poisoning Case," but nothing else. Perhaps Jakes wanted to keep it out of the news for now, but did that mean more arrests were coming?

The next morning was like waiting for a bomb to drop. Nobody else, not even John, seemed on edge, and Jakes didn't come around. At one point, Lawrence found me. "Is Perle coming by today?" He asked.

"She drove down to visit with her family," I responded.

"Oh, well, when you see her next, tell her that I found the extra teacup."

"You did? And?!"

"That's it," he replied. Then, he left without saying anything else.

Close to noon, I put down the novel I was reading and decided to go for a swim. After putting on my suit, robe, and Crocs, I went outside, towel in hand, and headed toward the swimming pool.

From behind, a voice called out.

"*Mon ami* Helen!"

"Perle," I exclaimed, with relief, and seizing her by both hands, I dragged her into the pool lodge. "I'm so glad to see you! I can barely believe what happened, but when do you think the news will spread?"

"My friend," replied Perle, "I do not know what you are talking about."

I felt a burst of impatience. "Dr. Blake's arrest, of course."

"Blake was arrested?"

"You hadn't heard?"

"No." But, pausing for a moment, she added, "Still, I'm not surprised, given what he was up to, and the scale of his operation. I'm surprised it took them so long."

"What are you talking about?"

Perle shrugged her shoulders. "Surely, it is obvious!"

"Not to me. No doubt I am very dense, but I don't see the connection to Emily's murder."

"Well, there isn't one."

"But they arrested him for murdering Emily!"

"What?" cried Perle, her eyes dancing. "Who told you that?"

"Well, no one exactly told me," I confessed. "But he was arrested."

"Oh, yes, but for his drug cartel."

"Drug cartel?" I gasped.

"Precisely."

"Not for poisoning Emily?"

"Not unless our friend Jimmy Jakes has lost his mind."

"But—but I thought you thought so too?"

Perle gave me one look, which conveyed both pity and amusement. She rubbed the back of her neck. "It is so warm and steamy here. Perhaps we could walk back to the lodge? Unless, you still wanted to swim?"

"No, that's okay." I went toward the door.

"Good. Then you change out of your Crocs. They are horrid footwear."

We strolled toward the main lodge. "Please explain it to me, Perle. Dr. Blake has a drug cartel?"

"Of sorts. He fancies himself a Robin Hood, and he illegally moves high-cost prescription drugs out through Thunder Bay, and then distributes them to people here, at a fraction of what they would normally pay. His methods are illegal, but I believe his heart is in the right place."

I thought for a moment. "Do you think Mary worked for him?"

"Perhaps," Perle answered. "I'm sure Jakes has looked into that connection."

We got back to the lodge, and I went upstairs to change. I put on leggings and a flannel shirt, of which Perle would probably disapprove, but I felt it was entirely appropriate apparel for the North Shore. I did change into soft leather sneakers, which were a step up from Crocs. I was combing my hair when there was a knock on my door.

"Come in." I expected Perle. But it was Mary.

"Oh, hello," I said, surprised. She'd never visited my room before.

"Hi. Do you have a moment?"

My stomach turned over. What now? Had she seen me behind that tree after all?

"Sure," I responded.

Mary took a deep breath. "I know there's a rumor spreading, but I don't hate Cynthia. As far as I'm concerned, she can stay as long as she wants."

"Oh." I laughed softly. "That's not what I was expecting you to say."

She cocked her head. "What *were* you expecting?"

"I don't know."

Mary met my eyes, and I could tell she was on to me. "Helen, I know how much you admire John. But there's a lot you don't understand about my marriage to him. Sometimes I think I should leave him. That perhaps our relationship has run its course."

My throat went dry. "I don't think you should tell me this, at least not before you speak to him about it."

"Right. Sorry." She turned around.

"Wait," I said, before she could walk out. "Did you hear about Dr. Blake?"

Mary pressed her lips together. "Of course. John told me this morning. He couldn't resist the satisfaction of seeing my face when he broke the news." She drew herself up, straightened her shoulders, and gave me a dismissive nod. Then she walked off.

I took a moment and a few deep breaths, and left my room as well. When I got downstairs, Evie and Perle were talking. I heard Evie say, "In a bag, at the back of his closet."

"What's going on?" I asked.

"Nothing," said Evie, and she hurried off.

"Perle." I stepped in front of her and beseeched her with my eyes. "Have you made up your mind about this crime?"

Perle tilted her chin, so far that her bun almost reached her collar. "Yes—that is to say, I believe I know how it was committed. But we shall see if Jakes arrives at the same conclusion."

"Aren't you going to tell him what you know?"

"Oh of course I will. But only if he asks me."

Perle caught me rolling my eyes, but she didn't react. Instead she said, "Oh, by the way, I saw Cynthia's pharmacy today, when I got back into town."

"Oh yeah? Did you come to any conclusions?"

"Only that many people had access to the locked cabinet, especially if they went through Cynthia."

"You would think that Jakes would look into that possibility," I said.

"I agree," said Perle. "But one thing does strike me. No doubt it has struck you too."

"What is that?"

"There is altogether too much strychnine about this case. This is the third time we have run up against it. There was strychnine-like herb in Emily's sleep powder. There is the strychnine sold across the counter for a supposed rat problem. Now we have more strychnine, conceivably handled by anyone in the house. It is confusing, and, as you know, I do not like confusion."

"Speaking of confusion, I nearly forgot. Lawrence told me to tell you that he found the extra teacup. He wouldn't elaborate on that, though."

Perle smiled.

"I suppose," I said, "you're not going to explain."

She stood and patted me on the arm. "*Mon ami* Helen, it will soon become crystal clear; I promise."

Before I could reply, Dorcas ran in, crying and wringing her hands. Mary heard the fuss and came downstairs. "What is it, Dorcas?"

"Oh, Mary! I don't know how to tell you—"

"What is it, Dorcas?" My heart leapt into my throat. I knew a bombshell was coming.

"They've arrested him—they've arrested Mr. Cavendish!"

"They arrested Lawrence?" I gasped.

I saw a strange look come into Dorcas's eyes.

"No. Not Lawrence—they arrested John."

Behind me, with a wild cry, Mary Cavendish fell heavily against me, and as I turned to catch her, I saw the quiet triumph in Perle's eyes.

ELEVEN

BUT HE'S INNOCENT

As they led John out, Mary promised to find him the best lawyer available. Then she gasped, "I love you!'" and cried when the police wouldn't let her hug her husband. I watched as the police car, with John inside, drove away. "But he's innocent," Mary said to me. "Surely you believe that, Helen?"

My thoughts were muddled, and I didn't know what to believe. Perle seemed to think he was guilty, and I was starting to believe that she was right about everything. If so, then I had to admit that I had no instinct, so how could I trust my gut on this one?

Yet, were my instincts wrong when I stood between John and that rioter? Did I risk my life to protect a man who'd one day murder his surrogate mother? Perhaps, but then the world I knew had turned upside down.

In the distance, Jakes stood on the beach, staring out at Lake Superior. "I'll see what I can find out," I said to Mary. "And I'll help John if I can."

I walked across the stone beach and stood near Jakes, hugging my thin flannel shirt to me. It did little to protect against the cool lake breeze. "You're still here," I stated, and it was neither a recrimination nor a compliment.

"I'll go soon. I still need to catalog some of the evidence back in the lodge. Otherwise, I think my work here is just about done."

"Only just about?" I asked. "You got your man."

"Do you mean Dr. Blake, or John Cavendish?"

"I meant John," I replied. "So, you were behind Blake's arrest?"

Jakes scratched his shiny, bald head. "Yeah. We'd been on to him for a while. Honestly, he's the reason the FBI was called in. We wanted to see if there was a connection, and if Emily, who'd just died mysteriously, and her son, who happened to be a state senator, knew about his drug cartel."

"Did they?"

Jakes' wide grin appeared. "You know I can't tell you that."

I nodded and was surprised when I felt tears forming. I swallowed them back. "I understand."

"Hey, are you okay?" Jakes reached out his hand, but I stepped away from his touch. The last thing I wanted to do was to play the damsel in distress. "John is my friend. And, I don't know … you and Perle seem sure that he's guilty, but to me, something doesn't add up."

"We found a pair of fake glasses, ones exactly like the ones Alfred wears, and a jar of gopher poison, in a bag that was shoved into the back of his closet." Jakes sighed. "I mean, I probably shouldn't have told you that. But between John's argument with Emily and his money problems, well, he has a motive. And now the evidence points in his direction, enough that we can make an arrest."

I said nothing, but simply stared out at the gray water.

Jakes stepped in close to me, and we stood, side by side. "I can't discuss the case with you anymore, Helen. I've already said too much. Perhaps you should tell Perle your concerns?"

"She'd dismiss them," I said.

"No. That's not true. Every time I ran into her when you weren't around, she'd go on and on about you. '*Mon ami* Helen is the best student I ever had.' I started to think she was trying to make me jealous. Or maybe she was playing matchmaker? Perle knows I need someone who will challenge me."

I abruptly turned, looking for signs of teasing in his eyes. But they only contained sincerity.

He sighed. "Anyway, when this case has been resolved, I hope it's okay if I maybe give you a call?"

Despite myself, I laughed. This confident, imposing man sounded so unsure. But when his face fell, I regretted my response. "Sorry," I said. "I wasn't laughing at you. Just at the idea …" I scrambled to improvise, "… at the idea of this case ever being resolved."

He squinted at me. "So, can I call you?"

"If and when we know who the real killer is, yes. Please do."

There was an electric moment when Jakes parted his lips, ever so slightly. Slowly, he leaned both in and down, like he might kiss me. With a sudden burst of desire, I realized how good it was to feel this way, to want someone other than Paul's mouth on mine, to be filled with something besides grief. But should I let him kiss me?

No. It was better to play the long game, which everyone at Styles (except me) knew how to do. Still, I couldn't rebuff him altogether. So, standing on my tiptoes, I abruptly raised my arms and captured him in a hug. He responded by wrapping his arms around my waist and gripping me tightly. I took a deep, happy breath before I reluctantly pulled away.

"I should go," I said. "I need to help the family however I can."

I stepped away and walked the tricky stone path back to the lodge. Halfway there, I changed course. Why not tell Perle what I thought? The worst she could do was laugh and insult me, and I'd endured that before. I went and knocked on her condo door. She answered immediately. I must have had a strange look on my face, because she said, *"Mon ami,* Helen. What is the matter?"

"Why didn't you tell me it was John?" I stepped past her and entered her condo. I was a bit angry, but not so much that I didn't pause to take my shoes off. Perle would go crazy if I tracked in dirt.

"Why do you *think* that I didn't tell you?"

I stood up straight now that my feet were bare. "Because he is my friend."

"Exactly."

"But Perle, don't you see? John *is* my friend, and I am, at least, a good judge of character."

Perle motioned me into the living room. I sat on the couch, and she sat in an armchair. "But Helen, is that true? Haven't you made a habit of trusting the wrong men?"

I winced, remembering how when Paul left me for another woman so soon after my miscarriage, I'd emailed Perle. *I loved him and I trusted him! I thought he was a good person, but I was wrong.* Now that line swam before my eyes, and it surely reverberated in Perle's mind.

"That's hardly fair," I said.

"Perhaps not," said Perle. "I apologize." She took a deep breath. "Okay, Helen. Explain it to me. Why is John innocent?"

"Because …" my mind wandered. I couldn't say, *Because he brought me coffee and cookies when I was sad,* or, *Because I believed his impassioned floor speeches about voting rights, gun control, and educational funding.* Even if that was part of it, Perle needed something more concrete. Then, it came to me.

"I briefly thought that Blake murdered Emily, and I tried to convince John. He didn't believe me. He said it made no sense because Blake didn't have a motive. He questioned other points of my argument as well. John knew I was working with you, and that I'd grown close to Jakes. This could have been his opportunity to pin the crime on someone other than himself. So, why didn't he take it?

Perle's forehead creased thoughtfully. "Yes, why indeed?" She reached for a deck of cards that sat on the side table next to her chair. Then, to my amazement, she took the cards out of their envelope, and solemnly began to build a card house.

Two cards balanced with another card laying horizontally across. My jaw dropped involuntarily, and she said at once:

"No, *mon ami*, I am not in my second childhood! I must steady my nerves, that is all. Card houses require absolute finger precision. With finger precision comes precision of the brain. And I've never needed that more than now!"

"So, then, you agree with me about John?"

With a great thump on the table, Perle demolished her carefully built house of cards.

"It is so frustrating, *mon ami!* I can build card houses seven stories high, but I cannot"—thump—"find"—thump—"the last link."

I didn't know what to say, so I held my peace, and she began slowly building up the cards again, speaking in jerks as she did so.

"It is done—so! By placing—one card—on another—with mathematical—precision!"

I watched the card house rising under her hands, story by story. She never hesitated or faltered. It was pure magic.

"You've got such a steady hand," I remarked. "I believe I've only ever seen your hand shake once."

"I must have been angry," Perle stated.

"Exactly! Don't you remember? It was when you discovered that Emily's computer was broken into and wiped clean, and that her briefcase had also been broken into. You stood by the mantelpiece, straightening the things on it and your hand shook like a leaf!"

But I stopped suddenly. For Perle, with a hoarse and inarticulate cry, swung her arm and again annihilated her masterpiece of cards. Then she put her hands over her eyes and swayed backward and forward, like a wounded animal.

"Perle, what is it? Are you having another hot flash?"

"No, no," she gasped. "Or, I don't know, perhaps I am. But—it is—that I have an idea!"

"Oh!" I exclaimed, very much relieved. "But you get ideas all the time."

"You don't understand! This time it is an epic idea! Stupendous! And you—*you*, my friend, have given it to me!"

She shot up, joined me on the couch, and kissed me warmly on both cheeks. Before I could recover, she was by the door, putting on her shoes. "We must go to the lodge," she said.

Her energy and intensity were contagious, so, without questioning why, I did as she said. When we got to the lodge's door, she swung it open and called out, "Inspector Jimmy Jakes! Are you still here? We must speak!"

THE LAST LINK

"I'm right here," Jakes said, coming around the corner. "What is it, Perle?"

Involuntarily, I smiled at seeing him.

"Ah, I am so glad you haven't driven back down to the cities yet. With your permission, I'd like to call a meeting in the lounge. Everyone must attend."

Jakes met my eye, and I shrugged. "Of course," he said. "Let's do it."

We set up chairs, and I told everyone to come down to the lounge. Soon the whole gang, minus John of course, was there. Perle even texted Alfred, and for reasons I did not understand, he arrived shortly after her summons.

"How did you get his number?" I whispered in Perle's ear.

"I asked him for it," she responded.

It was a familiar scene, not unlike before, when Perle explained Alfred's innocence to us all. They all sat in chairs that formed a semi-circle, and Jakes stood in the back. However, this time, I stood near him, rather than up in front, near Perle.

When Evie saw Alfred, she grunted. "I'm not staying if he's here!"

"No, no!" Perle went up to her and pleaded in a low voice, after a couple of moments, Evie relented. Now that everyone was assembled, Perle stood before us all with the air of a popular lecturer and bowed politely to her audience.

"As you all know, John Cavendish agreed to have me investigate this case. After Emily's tragic death, I immediately examined Emily's bedroom, which until then was kept locked, so it was exactly as it had been when the tragedy occurred. I found a fragment of green material, a stain on the carpet near the window, still damp, and an empty jar of sleep powder.

"First, the green fabric. It was caught between the door that joined Cynthia and Emily's rooms. I handed the fragment over to the police who did not consider it of much importance. But they didn't recognize it for what it was: a torn scrap of a green work shirt."

There was a murmur of excitement.

"Now there was only one person at Styles who wore a green work shirt. Therefore, it was Mary who entered Emily's room through the connecting door from Cynthia's room."

"But that door was bolted on the inside!" I cried.

"When I examined the room, yes. But we have only Mary's word for it, since she was the one who tried that particular door and said it was bolted. In all the confusion, she found a time to bolt that door. Also, the fragment corresponds exactly with a tear in Mary's shirt. And, at the inquest, Mary said that she heard, from her own room, the sound of the table falling by the bed. I tested that statement by stationing Helen down the hall, outside of Mary's door. I went to Emily's room, and while there, I," Perle made air quotes, "*accidentally* knocked over the table in question, but found that, as I had expected, Helen didn't hear a thing. This confirmed my belief that Mary was not in her own room, but in Emily's room shortly before she died."

I shot a quick glance at Mary. She was very pale but smiling.

After a dramatic pause, Perle read the room, and then she continued. "The question is, why?" People shifted and glanced at Mary, who kept her mouth shut. Perle went on. "She was looking for something and couldn't find it. Suddenly Emily woke up and had a seizure. Mary is startled and knocks over the scented candle that had been burning not long before, spilling wax on the carpet. She picks it up, and retreats to Cynthia's room, closing the door behind her. But it is too late! People have heard Emily's cries and are running down the hall. What can she do? Quick as thought, she hurries back to Cynthia's room, and starts shaking her awake. Everyone comes. They are all busily banging on Emily's door. It occurs to nobody that Mary hasn't arrived with the rest, but—and this is significant—I can find no one who saw her come from down the hall." She looked at Mary. "Am I right?"

Mary bowed her head. "Yes. And if it will help John, I'll make an official statement, describing the whole thing."

"The will!" cried Lawrence. "Then it was you, Mary, who destroyed the will?"

She shook her head, and so did Perle.

"No," Perle said quietly. "The person who destroyed that will was Emily herself!"

I was so confused. "But why would she destroy it, when she'd only made it that afternoon?"

"We have been backward in our thinking." Perle explained patiently, "Emily argued with John that afternoon, probably about the will. But the argument took place after, and not before the making of the will."

Everyone in the room made a collective sigh. "Let's go back," Perle said. "We know Emily and John argued. Dorcas said she heard something about 'a scandal between husband and wife.'" We know that Mary later argued with Emily as well. We assumed the argument and the 'marital scandal' was about Emily and Alfred. But not Mary. She was sure Emily had proof of her husband's infidelity."

"Huh?" Several of us said at once. Mary, silent, stared at her hands.

Perle tilted her chin. "Stay with me. There was a brief stretch of time, in between Emily's arguments with John and then with Mary, that she was alone. What happened? It had to be something unexpected, and something significant."

Next to me, Jakes cleared his throat. Was it a subtle urge for Perle to get to the point? Perle self-consciously paced a bit and continued. "I can only assume, but I believe that after the argument with John, Emily went searching through Alfred's desk to look for stamps. She had official documents that needed to be mailed by post, and Dorcas mentioned to me that she was out of stamps. While looking for the stamps, Emily found something incriminating, something she was not meant to see. Mary, after stewing a while, barged into Emily's office. She found her mother-in-law looking upset and holding a piece of paper. Mary demanded to see it, and when Emily refused, Mary assumed she was protecting her stepson. Mary was determined, and she felt sure that John was having an affair. She decided she had to get hold of that paper at all costs. She saw Emily put the paper in her briefcase and bring it up with her laptop that night, so Mary made her plans as only a woman driven desperate through jealousy could have done. Sometime in the evening she unbolted the door leading into Cynthia's room. Possibly she applied oil to the hinges, for I found that it opened quite noiselessly when I tried it. She waited until the early hours of the morning as being safer since no one would hear her move about her room at that time. She made her way quietly through Emily's room and into Cynthia's room."

Perle paused for a moment, and Cynthia interrupted. "Wouldn't I have woken up?"

"No, not if you were drugged," stated Perle.

Cynthia went pale. "Drugged?"

"You can't be serious," Lawrence cried.

"You remember"—Perle addressed us collectively again—"that through all the tumult and noise next door, Cynthia slept. So, either her sleep was feigned—which I did not believe—or her unconsciousness was induced by artificial means.

"That is why I examined all the teacups carefully, remembering that it was Mary who had brought Cynthia her tea the night before. I took a sample from each cup and had them analyzed—with no result. I had counted the cups carefully, in case one had been removed. Six people had tea, and six cups were duly found. I, unwillingly, admitted to myself I'd been wrong."

Perle's face flushed, and for a moment, I worried she was about to have another hot flash. But no, it simply pained her to admit to making a mistake.

"But then I discovered that tea had been brought in for seven people, not six, because Dr. Blake was there that evening. This changed everything, for there was now one cup missing.

"I was confident that the missing cup was Cynthia's, because all the cups I found contained sugar, which Cynthia never took in her tea. I was also curious about the cocoa cup from Emily's room, so I took it to be analyzed."

"But that had already been done by Dr. Blake," said Lawrence quickly.

"Not exactly. The analyst was asked whether strychnine was, or was not, present. He did not have it tested, as I did, for a narcotic."

Jakes shifted his weight. "For a narcotic?"

"Yes. The analyst's report stated that Mary administered a safe, but effective, narcotic to Emily in her cocoa."

"Wait," I said. "How? How did Mary get a narcotic in the first place, and how did she get it into Emily's cocoa? She used a Keurig machine."

Everyone looked toward Mary. Her shoulders sagged. "I had some leftover codeine after my oral surgery last winter. I dissolved it into the water bank of the Keurig machine. I also put some in Cynthia's tea"

Perle paused only a moment, to let that sink in, before she continued. "But poor Mary! Imagine how she felt when her mother-in-law is violently ill and dies, and immediately after she heard the word 'Poison'! Mary thought that what she gave was perfectly harmless, but for one terrible moment, she must have feared that Emily's death was her fault. She was seized with panic, and under its influence, she hurried downstairs, and quickly dropped the teacup and saucer used by Cynthia into a large brass vase, where it was discovered later by Lawrence. She didn't dare touch the remains of the cocoa because too many eyes were upon her. I can only imagine her relief when she realized Emily died by strychnine poisoning, and that the tragedy was not her fault."

At this point, our eyes were glazing over. As charitably as I could, I asked, "But what's the significance of all that?"

Perle shook her head at me, like she couldn't believe I had to ask. "*Mon ami,* Helen. We are now able to account for the symptoms of strychnine poisoning being so long in making their appearance. A narcotic taken with strychnine will delay the action of the poison for hours."

Perle paused. Mary looked up at her, the color slowly rising in her face. "Everything you said is true. It was the worst hour of my life." She turned to Cynthia, trembling. "I am so sorry I drugged you. I just had to find out what Emily was hiding. There's a certain … insanity that comes with the belief that your husband is unfaithful."

Cynthia narrowed her eyes at Mary. "Did you think that I was sleeping with John?"

Mary sucked in a breath. "I thought that maybe John was involved with you, or with Janet Raikes, or maybe both of you? I couldn't get the suspicion out of my mind."

"Why didn't you just ask me?" Cynthia replied.

Mary looked around the room. "Can we have this conversation later, in private?"

Cynthia nodded, and a tense silence followed, but thankfully it was quickly broken.

"Now I understand," said Lawrence, loudly changing the subject. "The drugged cocoa, taken on top of the poisoned tea, explains the delay."

"Exactly!" Perle pointed at Lawrence, like a teacher praising her prized student. "But was the tea poisoned, or was it not? Here, we have some confusion since Emily never drank it."

"What?" The cry of surprise was universal. Even Jakes shouted out his shock.

Perle suppressed a smile. She had us where she wanted us. "You remember that I mentioned a stain on the carpet in Emily's room? It smelled strongly of tea, and splinters of china were ground into the carpet. It became clear what happened. Emily reached for her tea, the table was knocked over, and so she decided to make herself some cocoa. But we know the cocoa contained no strychnine. The tea was never drunk. Yet the strychnine must have been administered between seven and nine o'clock that evening. What third medium was there—a medium so suitable for disguising the taste of strychnine that it is extraordinary no one has thought of it?" Perle looked around the room, and then, quite grandly, answered herself. "Her sleep powder!"

I gasped. "Do you mean that the murderer mixed strychnine into her sleep powder?"

"Exactly. The strychnine that killed Emily was added to the maqianzi, the herb that, if used in excess, can poison in the same way as strychnine. That was already in Emily's sleep powder prescription. The murderer simply added a bit more strychnine, *and* some bromide powder. This is important, before he was arrested, Dr. Blake confirmed to me that a bit of the powder introduced into the full bottle of sleep powder would effectively precipitate the strychnine and cause it to be taken in the last dose."

"Yes, of course," cried Cynthia. And Lawrence nodded along.

Jakes spoke up. "Can you explain? Those of us without medical or pharmaceutical backgrounds need help."

"Of course." Perle smiled. "Throughout the case, there's been evidence that the murder was intended to take place on Monday evening. But Emily didn't take her powder one night, so that the last—and fatal—dose was actually taken twenty-four hours later than had been anticipated by the murderer; and it is owing to that delay that the final proof—the last link of the chain—is now in my hands."

Amid breathless excitement, she held out a piece of paper that had clearly been ripped up and taped back together.

In the deathly silence, Perle cleared her throat and read:

Dearest Evie:

Don't worry, everything is all alright—only it will be tonight instead of last night. You understand. We can relax once the old woman is dead and out of the way. No one can possibly pin the crime on me. Your idea was genius! But we must lay low.

Evie's howl that was almost a scream broke the silence.

"You devil! How did you get it?"

A chair was overturned. Perle skipped nimbly aside. A quick movement on his part, and her assailant fell with a crash. Jakes and I rushed up to the front of the room to prevent anyone from escaping.

"Ladies and Gentlemen," said Perle, with a flourish, "let me introduce you to the murderer, Mr. Alfred Inglethorp!"

THIRTEEN

PERLE EXPLAINS

Almost immediately, the charges against John were dropped, and Jakes took Evie and Alfred into custody. When John walked through the door of Style's Lodge, Mary ran into his arms and gave him a passionate kiss.

"Let's give them some privacy," Perle suggested. "Walk me to my condo?"

The cool, fresh air was a welcome relief after the day's intensity. There was a strong breeze, and Lake Superior's waves crashed against the shore.

"I suppose I'll have to get back to work soon," I said.

Perle sensed my melancholy tone. "Are you sure you want to go back?"

"I don't have much of a choice."

"*Mon ami,* Helen, there is always time for a new path or a new choice. And you are young. The possibilities are endless, especially for someone as talented as you.

"How can you say that, when you chose to deceive me the whole time?"

"I did not deceive you, *mon ami.* At most, I permitted you to deceive yourself."

"Yes, but why?"

"Well, it is difficult to explain. You see, my friend, you have an honest nature and you do not conceal your true feelings. That makes you a gem. However, if I told you my suspicions, I knew that the first time you saw Alfred and Evie, you'd have inadvertently betrayed everything, and then we never would have caught them."

I rolled my shoulders back, trying to abate the tension building between my blades. "I think I'm a little more sophisticated than that."

"Ah, Helen." Perle turned toward me, widening her eyes. "Don't be angry. Without you, I would not have figured it out. Your insights into the people's hearts were invaluable. You have a beautiful nature, and that is precious."

It was a compliment, I'm sure, but still, I needed more. "So, you might say that my instincts were spot on. Or even that my instincts were a little *too* good?"

Perle laughed. "Yes."

"Well," I grumbled, a little mollified. "I still think you might have given me a hint."

"But I did, my friend. Several hints. You would not take them. Think now, did I ever say to you that I thought John Cavendish was guilty?"

I stepped on a large rock, and my ankle nearly turned. "No, but——"

"And" continued Perle, "at the beginning, didn't I say that I didn't want Alfred arrested *now*? That should have conveyed something to you."

"Do you mean you suspected him the whole time?" She sighed and gazed toward the cloudy sky. "Yes. It's always the husband, is it not?" She looked at me and arched an eyebrow. "Alfred seemed slippery. At first, I couldn't figure out his plan, but I knew he had one. And, he had the motive since he stood to gain the most from Emily's death."

"Yeah, but Evie didn't have a motive."

"Love was her motive."

"Huh?"

Perle let out a patient sigh. "*Mon ami,* Helen, Evie and Alfred were not cousins. Surely you figured this out? And they only pretended to hate each other, when really, they were in love. I expect they cooked up the whole scheme to kill Emily for her inheritance months in advance."

"Oh." I hadn't figured all that out, but I wasn't going to question Perle. I was just happy to hear that Alfred and Evie weren't actually cousins.

We reached Perle's condo. She'd left the door unlocked. I suppose, given her scrupulous, investigative mind, that meant she had a beautiful nature as well.

We walked in and headed straight for her living room. "But," I began, "for a while, you believed Alfred was innocent. When did you change your mind?"

"When I realized that the harder I tried to clear him, the harder he tried to get himself arrested."

I sat, but Perle remained standing. "I am hungry," she stated. "Would you eat cheese and crackers, if I put out a tray?"

"Yes, thank you."

"And I know it is the middle of the day, but I believe we should celebrate. I will also pour us some wine."

"Can I help?"

"Sit, *mon ami.*"

The kitchen was a mere few feet away. As she poured the wine and put cheese, crackers, and salami onto a tray, I increased my volume just a tad to say, "Wait a minute. Why did Alfred want to be arrested?"

"Because, as you know, once a man is acquitted, he can never be tried again for the same offense." I heard the *glug glug* of the wine being poured. "It was a clever idea! He is a man of method. He knew people would suspect him, so he prepared a lot of manufactured evidence against himself. Alfred *wanted* to be arrested. He would then produce his irreproachable alibi—and, hey presto, he was safe for life!"

Pearle brought in the tray of food and wine and placed it on the coffee table. She handed me a glass of wine and said, "Let's toast! Crime will be punished, and justice will be served!"

I toasted, drank the wine, but then I thought about things a bit too hard. I scrunched up my face, showing my confusion.

Perle, as always, could read my mind. "My poor friend! You have not yet realized that it was Evie who bought the strychnine?"

"Evie?"

"Who else? It was easy for her. She is tall, her voice is deep and manly, and Alfred helped her style the fake mustache."

"Okay, but I am still confused how exactly they knew about prolonging the strychnine poisoning," I remarked.

Perle munched on a cheese and cracker, over a plate of course. "My theory is this: Cynthia left one of her pharmacist textbooks around, when she was studying for the exam. Or, Evie simply did some internet research. She learned how to dissolve some bromide powder and strychnine into the sleep powder. What could be easier than quietly dissolving one or more of those powders into Emily's prescription? The risk is practically nil. The tragedy wouldn't take place until nearly two days later. If anyone saw either of them touching the medicine, they'd forget by the time Emily died."

I reached for my own cracker, careful not to scatter crumbs as I ate. "Can you go through the timeline?" I asked.

Perle nodded. "On Monday, at six o'clock, Alfred arranges to be seen by several people at a spot far removed from the village.

Evie made up a false story about him and Janet Raikes to account for his holding his tongue afterward. At six o'clock, Evie, disguised as Alfred, enters the chemist's shop, with her story about the rats, gets the strychnine, and writes Alfred's name. Everything is set, and Evie pretends to leave in a huff. It's not until Emily skips a night of the sleep powder that he slips up."

Perle pauses for dramatic effect. "Emily is out, and he sits down to write to Evie—"

I interrupt. "But, why would he write her a letter? Why not just text or email?"

Perle shrugs. "In this day and age, it is easier to not get caught when communicating by post. Paper can be burned, but most electronic communication will be retrieved, even if it's supposedly deleted. And, if Alfred and Evie rented a PO Box somewhere like Twin Harbors, the communication would arrive quickly. A letter without a return address would not leave much of a trail."

I considered this. "Okay, so Alfred writes to Evie?"

"Yes. He's afraid that she's in a panic over the non-success of their plan. He sits at his desk to write Evie a letter, but I assume Emily walked into the office unexpectedly. He quickly shoves the letter into his desk drawer, and then his instinct is to get away. He tells Emily that he's going for a walk. He doesn't think Emily will snoop inside his desk and find what he wrote.

"But this, as we know, is what happened. Emily reads it, and she knows there's something going on between Alfred and Evie, but she doesn't realize the extent of the danger that she's in. She decides to say nothing to her husband but determines to immediately destroy the will which she has just made. She keeps the fatal letter."

"So, Alfred forced open Emily's locked briefcase to find that letter?"

"Exactly," Perle responded. "And he ran an enormous risk trying to find it. It was the only proof that connected him to the crime."

"Okay, but why didn't he destroy the letter after he got hold of it?"

"Look at it from his point of view. There was a very brief time when he could have taken it, maybe five minutes immediately before our own arrival on the scene, for before that time people were milling around and would have seen him pass. He enters the room, unlocking the door with one of the other door keys—they were all much alike. He hurries to the briefcase—it is locked, and the keys are nowhere to be seen. That is a terrible blow to him, for it means that his presence in the room cannot be concealed as he had hoped. But he sees clearly that everything must be risked for the sake of that damning piece of evidence. Quickly, he forces the lock with a penknife, and turns over the papers until he finds what he is looking for.

"But he cannot keep that piece of paper on him. Once he leaves the room, he may be searched. If the paper is found on him, he is doomed. He must act quickly. Where can he hide this terrible slip of paper? The contents of the waste-paper-basket are kept and, in any case, are sure to be examined. There's no way to destroy it, and he doesn't dare keep it. He looks around, and he sees—what do you think, *mon ami?*"

I shook my head.

"The vase! He tears the letter into long thin strips, and rolling them up into spills, he thrusts them hurriedly in amongst the other spills in the vase on the mantle-piece."

"Incredible!" I exclaimed. "How did you figure it out?"

"I owe it to you."

"To me?"

"Yes. Do you remember telling me that my hand shook as I was straightening the ornaments on the mantelpiece?"

"Yes, but I don't see——"

"I'd already straightened them earlier that morning, when we had been together. And, if they were already straightened, there would be no need to straighten them again, unless, in the mean-time, someone else had touched them."

"Wow," I murmured, "so that explains it. You rushed into Emily's room, and found it still there?"

"Yes, and it was a race for time."

"But why did Alfred leave it there when he had plenty of opportunity to destroy it?"

"He was already under suspicion. He couldn't risk going back into Emily's room. They'd think he was tampering with the evidence, which he was. Then, Jakes and the police were around, and nobody could get through, including Evie."

I sat there, quietly absorbing all this information. Perle broke the silence. "I should add that it was your suspicions of Evie, that she was too intense in her hatred of Alfred, that made me see the light. Without you, I wouldn't have realized their plan to frame John."

I felt my cheeks warm at her praise. "I wonder why they chose John, and not Lawrence to frame."

"John stood to gain more from Emily's death."

"I suppose you're right. And now, only time will tell if he's implicated in the whole Dr. Blake debacle."

Perle waved that off. "Jakes said he doesn't think the charges will stick."

"Oh."

"I predict a happy ending for everyone but Alfred, Evie, and of course, Emily. But John and Mary will rekindle their romance, Lawrence will find the courage to tell Cynthia he loves her, and you will say yes when Jimmy Jakes calls to ask you out on a date."

I laughed. "How do you know so much?"

"*Mon ami,* Helen. Do you really need to ask?"

She stood and poured more wine into both of our glasses. "I think you and I make a good team. Now that my daughters are both at college, I have more time on my hands. I am considering starting my own PI firm. Perhaps you'd be interested in working together?"

My mouth dropped open, but I quickly snapped it shut. Of course I would say yes, but I couldn't seem over eager. "Perhaps," I replied. Then I smiled and lifted my glass. "To the possibilities."

Perle smiled. "May they be endless."

We clinked our glasses together and toasted the future.

THE END